The Story So Far...

After her father's death, Gemma Smith left the opal fields of the Outback for Sydney to find out the truth about her mother, and to sell her priceless discovery, a flawless black opal.

Fate introduced Gemma to Nathan Whitmore, a famous screenwriter, who offered her a reward for the gem, which had been stolen from Byron Whitmore, Nathan's adoptive father, twenty years before. Highly attracted by Gemma's vulnerability, Nathan also seduced and married her.

Gemma's life was changed forever, and she witnessed startling events in the Whitmore household, too: Nathan's wild-child adoptive sister, Jade, discovered happiness with Kyle Gainsford, while Melanie, the family housekeeper, let go of her traumatic past and married Royce Grantham. And just look at what had happened to Ava, Byron's ungainly, much younger sister! She had lost weight and had found Vince Morelli, the handsome, caring Italian of her dreams! But where did all that leave Gemma and Nathan?

There were so many doubts and rumors that emma couldn't ignore, including the disturbing ings Damian Campbell had told her about athan's troubled past.

Dear Reader,

Welcome to the fifth book in a new and totally compelling family saga, set in the glamorous, cutthroat world of opal dealing in Australia.

Laden with dark secrets, forbidden desires, scandalous discoveries and happy endings, HEARTS OF FIRE unfolds over a series of six books, until December. Beautiful, innocent Gemma Smith goes in search of a new life, and fate introduces her to Nathan Whitmore, the ruthless, talented and utterly controlled screenwriter and heir to the Whitmore opal fortune.

Throughout the series, Gemma will discover the truth about Nathan, seduction, her real mother and the priceless Black Opal. But, at the same time, in each novel you'll find an independent, fully developed romance that can be read on its own, revealing the passion, deception and hope that has existed between two fabulously rich clans over twenty tempestuous years.

HEARTS OF FIRE has been especially written by one of romance fiction's rising stars for you to enjoy—we're sure you will!

THE EDITOR

MIRANDA LEE

Scandals & Secrets

Harlequin Books

TORONTO • NEW YORK • LONDON
AMSTERDAM • PARIS • SYDNEY • HAMBURG
STOCKHOLM • ATHENS • TOKYO • MILAN
MADRID • WARSAW • BUDAPEST • AUCKLAND

ISBN 0-373-11778-7

SCANDALS & SECRETS

First North American Publication 1995.

PRINCIPAL CHARACTERS IN THIS BOOK

GEMMA SMITH-WHITMORE: on her father's death, Gemma discovers a magnificent black opal worth a small fortune, and an old photograph that casts doubt on her real identity. In search of the truth about her mother, and a new life, she goes to Sydney, where she is seduced by, and then married to Nathan Whitmore.

NATHAN WHITMORE: adopted son of Byron Whitmore, Nathan is a talented screenwriter and playwright. After a troubled childhood and a divorce, Nathan is utterly ruthless and controlled. Will he ever be the loving, caring husband of whom Gemma has dreamed?

CELESTE CAMPBELL: head of the Campbell Jewelry empire, Celeste is rumored to have had numerous affairs with younger men. Celeste's beauty and business acumen make her a woman not to be toyed with—*she* does the toying. But her predatory exterior hides a broken heart for an old love that refuses to die....

BYRON WHITMORE: patriarch of the Whitmore family, he is a strong, dynamic figure, whose unhappy, loveless marriage came tragically to an end. Secretly very sensual, he did once come close to a woman, but his ambition was greater than his desire....

DAMIAN CAMPBELL: younger brother of Celeste, Damian abuses his position as sales and marketing manager in the Campbell Jewelry empire, as he is only interested in self-gratification and sexual pleasure. He doesn't care whom he hurts in their pursuit.

LENORE LANGTRY: talented stage actress, ex-wife of Nathan Whitmore and mother of Kirsty, Lenore has finally found love with top solicitor Zachary Marsden, though she still maintains a close relationship with Nathan.

AVA WHITMORE: Byron's much younger sister, Ava has blossomed and is now engaged to Vince Morelli, the owner of a gardening and construction business.

A NOTE TO THE READER:
This novel is one of a series of six set in the glamorous, cutthroat world of Australian opal dealing. It is the author's suggestion, however, that they be read in the order written.

FAMILY TREE

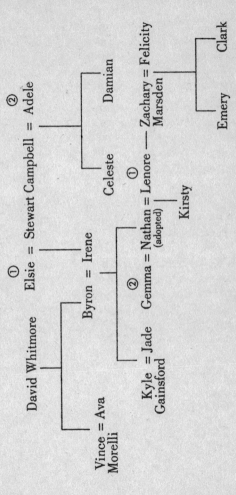

CHAPTER ONE

CELESTE was turning for her twentieth lap when a glimpse of male legs standing at the end of the pool brought her to a gasping halt, water-filled eyes snapping upwards.

'Good God, Damian,' she said irritably once she'd caught her breath and found her feet. 'You frightened the life out of me.'

Her brother laughed. 'Nothing and no one can frighten the life out of you, Celeste. What on earth did you think I was? A rapist?' He laughed again. 'I would pity any poor rapist who set his sights on you, sister, dear. I know who it'd be ending up on his back.'

Celeste flashed her brother a coolly reproachful glance as she stroked over to the wall, intuition telling her he was referring to her reputation as a man-eater, not complimenting her on her martial arts skills. Damian delighted in delivering sarcastic little barbs her way. In that respect he was very much like Irene.

Dismay and irritation mingled to rattle Celeste momentarily. If there was one person she didn't like thinking about it was her half-sister. Irene's death last year might have lessened the feelings of hostility and hatred Celeste had harboured against Irene all these years, but thinking about her inevitably led to thinking about another person, who was unfortunately very much alive.

'What do you want, Damian?' she snapped, her nerves suddenly on edge. 'It's not like you to surface on a Saturday till at least mid-afternoon. When you come home on a Friday night at *all*, that is.'

Her brother did not have a monopoly on sarcasm, Celeste realised with a twinge of conscience. Not that

Damian was capable of being hurt by such remarks. If anything, he seemed to enjoy any allusion to his decadent lifestyle.

Damian was a lost cause in Celeste's opinion. Spoilt, selfish and lazy, he was also far too good-looking for his own good. When he'd been younger, she'd made excuses for his wild behaviour, hoping he might grow out of being reckless and irresponsible, especially when it came to the opposite sex. But twenty-nine saw him as a playboy of the worst kind. Celeste was appalled at how many happy marriages he had destroyed. What a pity the wives never saw the wickedness behind that boyish smile and those magnetic black eyes!

If Celeste had had her way, she would have tossed Damian to the four winds ages ago and forced him at least to fend for himself. That might have given him a bit of character. But he was the apple of their mother's eye, and Adele had ignored all her daughter's advice when it came to her 'baby'. She'd insisted Damian be given a position in the family company, for which he was paid a salary far and above his contribution to Campbell Jewels, a salary which never seemed to meet his ever-increasing needs. Only last week, he'd approached Celeste for a loan, which she'd given him on the condition it was the first and last time.

'I hope you haven't come here looking for more money,' she added tartly as she levered herself out of the pool and stripped her cap off. Long tawny blonde waves tumbled over her forehead and eyes. Celeste combed her hair back off her face with her fingers before walking over to pick up a towel and start drying herself. 'If you have, you're wasting your time.'

Damian lowered himself on to one of the cane loungers and surveyed his sister with a curious mixture of dislike and admiration.

For a female rising forty, she was still a hot-looking bird. Of course she spent a fortune on her face and hair, and she worked the hell out of her body to keep it looking like that, without an ounce of extra flesh, every muscle toned and honed to perfection.

She was not to his taste, however, either physically or
personality-wise. Celeste was as hard as her body. He
liked his women soft, in all respects. And he preferred
brunettes, especially one particular brunette with big innocent brown eyes, the most luscious body and the
sweetest of smiles.

Damn, but he couldn't wait for the delectable Mrs
Nathan Whitmore to fall into his hands. They said everything came to those who waited but he was getting sick
and tired of waiting for Gemma to wake up to the sort of
man that husband of hers was. Maybe he would have to
think of some way he could give the situation a little
push...

Meanwhile, he was about to relieve his boredom by
giving his darling sister a different kind of push. Hell, but
he was going to enjoy relaying the news he'd found out
last night.

When Celeste saw Damian's mouth pull back into a
wickedly smug smile, a prickle of alarm shivered down
her damp spine.

'You'd like for me to have come crawling, wouldn't
you?' he said silkily, linking his hands behind his head
and crossing his ankles with an air of arrogant inso-
lence. 'You like having men suck up to you. It makes you
feel all-powerful. That's one of the reasons why you only
screw around with younger men. Because they grovel
better, and they're easier to control.'

Celeste's mouth dropped open for a second before it
snapped shut. Underneath his nasty delivery and under-
standably inaccurate assumptions, Damian *was* right
about her enjoying power over the male of the species.
That was one of her rewards for staying alive, for picking herself up from the edge of insanity and suicide, and
choosing to survive. It felt good to have men jumping to
obey her every whim and want, having them bow and
scrape. The days of her ever having to be afraid of a man,
or in having them control any aspect of her life, were long
over.

Or so she had believed. Till recently.

'What a delicate turn of phrase you have, Damian,' she said drily, needing a few moments to regain her composure after such a disturbing train of thought.

He laughed. 'Since when did you take offence at calling a spade a spade? You don't give a damn what people think of you, Celeste. You never have.'

Celeste frowned at this dig at the way she'd lived her life over the past decade or so, especially her uncaring attitude to scandal and gossip. It was true that she'd deliberately fuelled her reputation as a man-eater, publicly parading a long line of toy-boy companions for the gossip-mongers and tabloids to report.

What the general public did not know—or even her own brother—was that not once, during that time, had she actually been to bed with any of those young studs. Oh, yes, she'd flirted openly with them, especially when the cameras had been close. She'd allowed them to take her to highly publicised premieres, charity balls, the races and any other function where her photo was likely to be taken and printed, complete with partner.

Most of her supposed lovers had been independently wealthy playboy types from society families around Sydney. Some, however, had been employees—her personal assistant and chauffeurs were always young, male and handsome—whom she outwardly treated much more intimately than their position warranted. Amazing how quickly rumour escalated such relationships into tempestuous affairs.

Celeste suspected the men themselves lied about their conquests of the infamous female head of Campbell Jewels. Perhaps their male egos prompted them to feed the gossip about her reputedly voracious sexuality, each one in turn thinking they were the only one not to succeed in getting her into bed.

Celeste had never been bothered by any of this before. She had revelled in it all, finding some kind of weird vengeance in the knowledge that there was one particular person whom her scandalous reputation might hopefully hurt. She used to like to picture his face when he read or heard the latest gossip about her. She would imagine him hating her, yet still wanting her at the same time.

Thinking about his ongoing unrequited desire evoked an inner satisfaction that soothed the savage beast lurking within her heart.

Or it had. Till she'd taken herself off to the Whitmore Opals ball a few weeks back and come face to face with that unrequited desire, only to find out that her own desire for Byron Whitmore was still there, just as unrequited as his, and just as strong as ever.

Celeste had been utterly thrown. She'd been so sure she would never feel any desire for any man ever again, let alone the man who'd been the instigation of all her pain and anguish. Suddenly, that night, her much vaunted control over her life had been in danger of slipping away.

Any imminent disintegration had been temporarily staved off, however, by the most unlikely circumstances: an attempted robbery.

The prize for the thieves was to have been the Heart of Fire, a magnificent uncut black opal, the auction of which had been advertised as the highlight of the ball.

When she'd first heard news of the auction on the grapevine, she'd tried dismissing the thought that this could be the same opal which had played such an unfortunate part in her life over twenty years before, but once she saw it for herself on display in the Regency store windows all sorts of tortuous thoughts and futile hopes had forced her to walk back into the lion's den and confront the past as she had never confronted it before. In the flesh.

The results had been horrendous. Not only was she shattered by the realisation that she still wanted Byron in a sexual sense, she had also stupidly forked out two million dollars for an opal she couldn't even bear to look at. She hadn't even been to elicit any real information about the circumstances of the Heart of Fire's reappearance, Byron having answered her query with some slick lie about it turning up in some old dead miner's things at Lightning Ridge and being returned to him. As if anyone would just hand over a two-million-dollar opal!

Celeste had been in a most uncharacteristic mental turmoil that night when the balaclavaed robbers made their unexpected appearance. When one grabbed her as hostage, she'd been momentarily at a loss, obeying his commands and weakly going with him like a lamb to the slaughter, till some brutal manhandling had snapped her out of her submissive fog, revitalising her bitter determination never to surrender any of her self to any man in any way ever again, either emotionally or physically.

Out of the blue, she'd struck back, using the self-defence skills she'd learnt many years before, felling her assailants with two quick kicks. With hindsight, she almost felt gratitude to those brutes for bringing back horrific memories which in turn had renewed her fighting spirit.

Suddenly, she'd felt strong again, strong enough to defy this unwanted weakness of still wanting Byron Whitmore in a sexual sense. When fate placed her in his insidious presence once again a few days after the ball, she had delighted in deliberately courting his disgust in an appalling display of over-the-top flirtation with her chauffeur.

Unfortunately, her outrageous behaviour had backfired on her in a couple of ways. Firstly, the chauffeur had been inspired to take liberties later that evening and she'd had to fire him. But the second and more disastrous outcome was that this time Byron's obvious contempt had unaccountably *distressed*, instead of soothed her.

Celeste had eventually pulled herself together to the point where Byron ceased to fill her thoughts on a daily basis. But she certainly wasn't looking forward to confronting him again next Monday at the trial of the ringleader of the robbers, where they were both witnesses.

'Is this your version of the silent treatment?' Damian drawled in a derisive tone. 'If so, I find it incredibly boring.'

'Say what it is you have to say, Damian,' she answered sharply. 'I'm not in the mood for any of your sick little games.'

'*Moi*? Play sick games? Never!' His laughter grated on her already stretched nerves.

'Damian,' she rebuked. 'Get on with it!'

His hands dropped back to his sides and he sat up, a petulant expression on his too handsome face. 'You always spoil my fun.'

'Your idea of fun is not my idea of fun.'

'Really? I always thought it was. I like a bit of young stuff myself.'

Celeste's chin came up and she eyed her brother with distaste. 'I'm going over to the house. I have other things I'd rather do than stand here freezing to death.'

'What?'

'What do you mean, *what*?'

'I mean what else have you got to do? After all, you haven't found a new young stud to fill your leisure hours yet, have you? You know, Celeste, you never did tell me why you fired Gerry. I mean, I do realise it's rather clichéd—and a tad tacky—for the rich lady employer to have her chauffeur perform extra services but he did seem well equipped for the job.'

Celeste was appalled at the fierce heat that raced up her neck and into her cheeks. Blushing had never been her style but her newly sensitised self was suddenly finding the picture she had painted of herself over the years not only embarrassing but almost obscene. When hadn't she seen what she was doing? Where had her pride disappeared to? Clearly, her hatred of Byron and men in general had warped her so much that she didn't care what *anyone* thought of her.

But suddenly, she did. Dear God, she did...

'Well, well, well,' Damian drawled. 'Whatever did Gerry do? I would have thought he was a very straight young fellow. Did he try something a little more... adventurous? Is that it?'

'Don't be disgusting, Damian,' she snapped. 'I simply decided I didn't need a chauffeur any longer.'

'I see. So you have another gorgeous young hunk to tease Byron Whitmore with, do you?'

Celeste gasped before she could stop herself.

'You thought I didn't know?' Damian's smile was pure malice as he stood up and walked towards her. 'Silly Celeste. Didn't you know Irene always told me everything? I know all about your encounters with our dear sister's husband. Whoops, *half*-sister. Though he wasn't her husband the first time, was he? Merely her boyfriend.'

'He was not,' Celeste choked out, her head whirling with Damian's disclosure. 'Irene and Byron were not going out when I first met him. I was on work experience at Whitmore's. She didn't start going out with Byron till after I went back to boarding-school. I didn't try to take Byron away from Irene. She took him away from me!'

'And what of later, Celeste?' Damian said in a low, smarmy voice. 'He was her husband then, wasn't he?'

Celeste closed her eyes and shuddered.

'Yet you made love to him, didn't you?' Damian taunted softly. 'You had to have him, no matter what...'

Celeste's eyes opened, huge and haunted. 'Yes,' she confessed brokenly. 'Yes...'

'You callous bitch,' he said with so much venom that Celeste was stunned.

She shook her head. 'You don't understand how it was.'

He laughed. 'Oh, I understand only too well. We're all tarred with the same brush. Irene... You... Me... We take after dear Papa, which makes us not good people to cross. We want what we want and God help anyone who gets in our way. You and Irene wanted the same man. A cat fight was inevitable, but the only one who came out on top was Byron. Literally.'

'You're disgusting!'

'That's the pot calling the kettle black, surely.'

'It wasn't like Irene said. I didn't set out to seduce Byron. I didn't set out to do *anything*!' Anger that she was having to defend her morals to Damian, of all people, had her whirling away and dragging on the towelling robe that she'd brought with her. Flicking her hair over her shoulder, she turned back to face her brother with a steely expression on her face. 'I do not wish to discuss what happened with Byron in the past. It's dead and gone as Irene is dead and gone.'

'Really, Celeste? Are you saying you don't feel a thing for Byron any more, that he hasn't been your silent sexual prey all along?'

Outrage at both Damian and her own stupid feelings rose in her breast. 'I detest Byron Whitmore!' she lashed out. 'I wouldn't let him touch me if he was the last man on earth!'

'No kidding. Then it won't bother you that he's about to be married again.'

Celeste could no more stop the blood from leaving her face than she could the daggers of dismay that stabbed into her heart. She clutched the robe around her and did her level best not to sway on her feet, or look anything other than coldly indifferent. With a supreme effort of will, she somehow found a wry smile and a semblance of composure. 'Is that so?' she drawled. 'And who's the unlucky lady?'

Damian seemed disconcerted by her quick recovery. Clearly, he'd wanted to distress her, wanted to twist those daggers. His black eyes were still watchful on her, waiting for her to betray her feelings, but this only hardened Celeste's resolve to keep them to herself. If she was stupid enough still to feel anything for that holier-than-thou hypocrite, then the last thing she was going to do was show it or admit it. That would betray everything that had sustained her all these years.

'Her name is Catherine Gateshead,' Damian informed her sourly.

'And how did you come across this priceless information?' Celeste thought her tone was perfect. Just a little sarcastic, and a lot bored.

'A friend of hers told a friend of mine they were going to announce their engagement at Byron's fiftieth birthday party last night. It seems they've been quite a hot item for quite some time.'

Celeste battled to control a whole host of reactions, not the least of which was shock at hearing Byron's age. Fifty! He didn't look fifty. Clearly, he wasn't acting as

though he was fifty, either, she thought bitterly. Still, he'd
always been a highly sexed man and Irene *had* been dead
for nearly a year.

'And how old is this Catherine person?' she asked as
nonchalantly as she could manage.

Damian's smirk suggested he'd picked up on her ten-
sion. 'A good few years younger than you, dear sister.
And smashing-looking, I'm told.'

Celeste threw her brother a savage look and he
laughed.

'Jealousy can be an ugly thing. Not that you've got
anything to worry about, Celeste. No woman can hold a
candle to you when you put your mind to it. I'll never
forget the look on that bastard Whitmore's face when
you swanned into the Regency ballroom recently in that
dress. God, he couldn't keep his eyes off you. Not that I
blame him. That was some dress.'

Celeste cringed at the memory of the aforesaid dress.
She hadn't realised, till she was making her way down the
centre of the ballroom and caught a glimpse of herself in
one of the mirrored walls, how that dress looked from a
distance. The skin-coloured material and tightly fitted
style gave the illusion of nudity, the selected beading
marking out a provocative outline around her nipples and
crotch. Up close in the boutique, it had not looked so
scandalously revealing. Still, under Byron's critical gaze,
she'd had no alternative but to carry off the outrageous
outfit with panache or be left looking a fool.

'It was perfectly obvious to anyone with a brain in their
head,' Damian was raving on, 'that you've only got to
click your fingers his way and he'd drop Catherine
Whatsername as though she has a contagious disease.
Alternatively, you could have some real fun and wait till
he married the silly bitch, then move in for the ultimate
kill. A married Byron seems to bring out your best hunt-
ing instincts.'

Celeste amazed herself by not reacting visibly to
Damian's crude and inflammatory remarks. Her expression remained remarkably cool, as was her laugh. 'I think
you're confusing me with yourself, brother dear. You're

the one who's always running after married people. I prefer my bed partners both single and decidedly younger than fifty. I don't think Byron Whitmore fills the bill, do you?'

Retying the sash on her robe, Celeste picked up her towel and pushed past her brother, striding confidently towards the door. Damian scowled after her, irritated by his lack of success at stirring up trouble. What he didn't see was the grey pallor in his sister's face as she left the pool-house, or the haunted look in her eyes. Neither could he guess at the storm of emotion gathering in her heart, nor her lack of confidence in her ability to deal with any of it.

Celeste headed across the lawns and up the stone steps to the back of the house, blinking madly as she went. I do not care about Byron Whitmore, she kept saying to herself. I do not care what he does or where he goes or whom he marries. I do not care!

Celeste swept into the huge kitchen and put on the kettle for a cup of coffee. By the time she was sipping its soothing warmth, she was almost her old self again.

Till she suddenly remembered the trial on Monday.

Her head dropped into her hands, her stomach instantly churning.

'Oh, God...'

CHAPTER TWO

THE taxi sped off, leaving Gemma standing on the pavement with her suitcase at her feet. She was smiling to herself.

Nathan was going to get the shock of his life when she walked in. He thought she was out in good old Lightning Ridge, patiently awaiting the Monday afternoon flight back to Sydney. Instead, here she was, home a day early, the lucky passenger on a private jet chartered by an American couple staying at her motel.

The McFaddens had dropped in on the opal-mining town as part of a whirlwind tour of the outback of Australia, and, not finding the dust, flies and heat to their liking, had decided to head for Sydney posthaste. When Gemma had told them over breakfast this morning in the dining-room that she wished she were back home in Sydney as well, they'd offered her a lift. Delighted, she'd accepted, and here she was!

A glance at her watch showed it had only just passed one in the afternoon.

For a few seconds, she regretted that her trip back to Lightning Ridge had been so unrewarding in the matter of finding anything out about her missing mother. Perhaps she should have stayed the extra day and come back on the Monday as originally planned.

In all honesty, she hadn't tried all that hard, had she? One short interview with Mr Gunther—her dead father's only friend in Lightning Ridge—and one afternoon spent talking to the miners who'd just happened to drop into the pub. Neither would qualify as an in-depth investigation. Was it that underneath she was afraid of

the truth? Or of finding out that Nathan was right? Some
people's pasts were better off left there.

Still, the trip back to where she'd grown up had made
Gemma appreciate the life she had made for herself now
in Sydney. She had an interesting job selling opals to an
exclusive clientele in Whitmore's glamorous store in the
Regency Hotel. She was married to Sydney's most successful playwright who also just happened to be the most
handsome, sexiest man who'd ever drawn breath. And
soon she was going to start having the family she'd always wanted.

Her big brown eyes melted as she thought of her husband, and their phone conversation last Friday night.
That had been less than two days ago, but it seemed like
an eternity. She'd done exactly as he'd suggested and
thrown away her pills. Then she'd done the second thing
he'd wanted: come home.

Smiling a very female smile, she extracted her keys
from her carry-all handbag, picked up her suitcase and
walked over to the security door of the four-storey
building that housed their apartment. On the top floor,
their unit had a lovely view of Elizabeth Bay and, while
Gemma called it home for now, she knew she wouldn't
want to bring up a child, or children, in such a contained
and restricted environment. She would want a house and
a big back yard with a dog in it, a dog she would call
Blue.

Gemma's heart squeezed tight as she thought of that
moment out at the Ridge yesterday when she'd visited
Blue's grave. He was buried not far from the dugout
she'd been brought up in, on a small hillock he used to lie
on sometimes. She hadn't been able to stop the sudden
welling-up of emotion nor the flood of tears that had
streamed from her eyes. Now, as she turned the key and
let herself into the building, she felt those tears pricking
at her eyes again.

She would have brought Blue to Sydney with her if
she'd had the chance. But some rotten swine had poi-
soned him while she'd been at her father's funeral. She'd

been shattered when she found his body, seemingly more
upset over her dog's death than her father's.

Gemma felt a stab of guilt at that memory, frowning
as she carried her case inside the cool foyer and shut the
door behind her. Going back to Lightning Ridge had
dredged up memories she would rather have forgotten.
Yes, Nathan *was* right. One's happiness lay in the future, not the past. Her future and her happiness lay in her
marriage to Nathan, in their having a family together.

A determined expression momentarily thinned
Gemma's full mouth. If Nathan thought she was going
to stop at one baby, he was very much mistaken. She'd
hated not having any brothers and sisters, hated not
having a mother *and* a father. No child of hers was going to go through life feeling deprived and different, as
she had done. Her children would have every advantage
she could give them.

Gemma's mouth suddenly relaxed into a quietly rueful smile.

Just look at me, getting all carried away and serious.
Thinking too far ahead was as bad as spending all one's
energy worrying about the past. My first priority is being happy here and now—and in getting pregnant with
my *first* baby. Still, if Nathan's mood on the phone the
other night was anything to go by then the latter
shouldn't take too long.

Gemma hurried over to press the lift button on the
wall, her heart racing excitedly as she thought of what
was in store for her upstairs.

The lift doors whooshed back and she stepped inside
the empty compartment, pressing number four and
waiting impatiently for them to shut again.

Actually, she and Nathan hadn't made love for ages.
Not that Nathan hadn't wanted to. He *always* wanted to.
But some recent and rather shocking allegations about
Nathan's sexual history had played on her mind, and
she'd begun making excuses not to make love with her
husband. Even after being assured by an independent
source that the most shocking of these allegations was
untrue, she'd still found herself acting very negatively in

the bedroom. Nathan had been remarkably patient with her, and she aimed to reward that patience in full tonight.

Maybe I'll fall pregnant straight away, Gemma thought excitedly as the doors shut and the lift began to rise.

Probably not, she conceded, but it felt wonderfully warming to think about the possibility. It would give added meaning to what had previously been little more than a physical intimacy between them. Gemma held high hopes that having a baby together would bring about the emotional bonding with Nathan that she'd always felt was missing in their relationship.

With spirits high and pulse galloping, she stepped out of the lift on the fourth floor, eager to have her husband's arms around her, to have him kiss her as he'd kissed her at the airport the other day. Too bad if he was deeply involved with his writing. She was going to insist he leave it and give her his full attention. No doubt he would be holed up in his study, his handsome face buried in the computer screen. But nothing was going to save him from being seduced today. Nothing!

Gemma's grin faded to a frown as she opened their apartment door. Nathan's raised voice was coming through the closed double doors that led into the livingroom, sounding so impassioned that Gemma was shocked into stillness, her hand on the doorknob, her case still in the hallway outside. His next words came crystal-clear to her startled ears, and their content staggered her.

'So what if it was just sex last night?' Nathan scoffed angrily. 'And the night before. When has it ever been anything other than just sex between us?'

Gemma paled, her hand tightening over the knob as Lenore's voice flung a furious reply.

'When has it ever been anything else but just sex for you with *any* woman?'

Nathan laughed.

Despite her being already frozen with shock and horror, that cold laughter chilled Gemma to the bones.

'You think I didn't love you that night all those years,' Lenore swept on, 'when we made a baby together? You think that was only sex for me?'

'I *know* it was.' Scornfully.

'You bastard!'

'Nothing is to be achieved by calling names. Why don't you come over here and stop being a fool? Besides, you can hardly flounce out of here in a temper. You're not properly dressed.'

Gemma had to stuff a fist into her mouth to stop an anguished groan from escaping.

A muffled groan did find its way through those hideous doors, however, and Gemma thought she would die.

'I should never have let you talk me into coming here,' Lenore cried. 'I should never have let you touch me. You've always been bad news for women. God, but I hate you.'

'Shall we see how much?' he taunted.

'No, don't! Oh ... oh, God, I'm hopeless ...'

Gemma couldn't stand another second of such emotional torture, but the wild urge to burst in on them and create an embarrassing scene was superseded by feelings of pained pride. Why should she humiliate herself in front of two such shameless creatures? They wouldn't really care, except in how being caught out would affect their cruelly selfish and amoral lives.

But oh, God, the betrayal hurt as she'd never been hurt before. Nothing compared with the vice-like pain gripping her heart, nor the wintry emptiness within, as though her soul had been sucked dry by some huge emotional vacuum cleaner.

Gemma somehow managed to close the door, hoist her carry-all up on to her shoulder and pick up her suitcase. She didn't take the lift. She went down the fire stairs, quite slowly, each shuddering step like a death-kneel, her mind disbelieving of how quickly her excited happiness had been changed to despair.

Tears filled her eyes and flooded over, running down her cheeks. She didn't stop to wipe them away. Neither did she stop going down those steps. If she did, she would surely sag down into a wretched impotent huddle, and once she did that she would not have the energy or the courage to do anything or go anywhere. Nathan might accidentally find her there and she couldn't bear to hear the lies he was sure to come up with to explain what she'd overheard.

Gemma exited the building and turned to walk up the streets and around the corner, no real destination in mind. She just wanted to get as far away from Nathan and Lenore as she could. The act of walking was a salvation in itself, for having to put one foot in front of the other had a kind of robotic comfort. Gradually, the breeze dried the tears on Gemma's cheeks and she felt the pieces of her shattered soul gradually reassemble into something that was capable of making decisions.

Not that she was whole again. Her heart would never be whole again, she recognised bleakly. It would remain broken, but a type of glueing together was taking place as she walked, her bewildered despair giving way to the human survival technique of cynicism and anger.

You shouldn't be surprised, Gemma, a bitter voice berated. You had plenty of clues that Nathan hadn't married you for love, no matter what he claimed. True love does not keep its emotional distance, nor harbour dark secrets. It is open and trusting and warm and wonderful. Nathan, on far too many occasions, was secretive and distrusting and cold and downright wicked. Look at the way he enslaved your senses, turned you into little more than a sexual puppet. If he's been patient with you lately, it was because he had other fish to fry. He didn't need to make love to you because he was having an affair with Lenore!

And you suspected as much. Go on, admit it, you stupid little idiot! Underneath you were worried about the time he was spending with Lenore but in the end you chose to ignore it, because you wanted to believe in his love, wanted to keep pretending.

As for Lenore...

Now that the initial shock was over and she was thinking more clearly, Gemma was stunned to find she didn't feel quite so angry with Nathan's ex-wife. In fact, she almost felt sorry for her. If Lenore hated Nathan, as she said, then that was because she was also still in love with him. Gemma could well understand a woman loving and hating Nathan at the same time. She certainly did right at this moment. But at least the hate part seemed to clear one's vision of the man he really was. Lenore didn't sound as though she was under any illusions. Neither was Gemma any more. Just to love Nathan was to become a fool, there was no doubt about that. A blind fool!

Gemma looked back over all the warnings she'd been given about Nathan, the warnings she had naïvely ignored. Instead, she'd stupidly gone into a marriage based on nothing but the physical. His wanting her to have a baby was the one thing that she didn't quite understand. There again, men had babies all the time with women they didn't love. Maybe it was a matter of ego, of wanting to replicate their genes, or of wanting to keep the women under their control.

Nathan had demonstrated a jealousy and possessiveness over her from the start, suggesting that, while he might not love her, he did like 'owning' her. Since their marriage, he'd moulded her into the sort of wife that suited him, a sexually submissive little doll whom he could dress as he fancied, parade in public on his arm, then bring home and make love to as he pleased.

Well, he wouldn't be 'making love' to her any more, she vowed with an intense bitterness that kept the despair at bay. Their marriage was over as of this moment. She would never go back to him. Never ever!

Gemma strode on, around the next corner, heading towards she knew not what. But the ramifications of the decision she had just made were not long in sinking in. Would Byron give her the sack once he found out she'd left his precious adopted son? Even if he didn't, where was she going to live now? She had no real friends, no one she could turn to, except perhaps...

Damian had said she could rely on him if ever she needed a friend.

Gemma slowed her step. Why was she so loath to call Damian Campbell? Was it just pride that was stopping her, or something more complex than that? Nathan's own warnings about his enemy no longer held water, did they? One couldn't believe a thing he said. And yet . . .

Gemma sighed her confusion, halting completely on the pavement, putting the suitcase down. Momentarily, she closed her eyes, the events of the day threatening to overwhelm her. She felt so alone, so alone and so wretched. Tired too. Yes, suddenly, she felt dreadfully tired. Emotional exhaustion, she supposed.

Opening her eyes, she glanced around and there, on the next corner, stood an old hotel. What she needed was a quiet place to lie down. Somewhere she could simply sleep for a while. Nathan was not expecting her back in Sydney till the following afternoon. He was not expecting her to call tonight. This gave her over twenty-four hours to decide what action she was going to take. Wearily, Gemma picked up her suitcase again and began walking in the direction of the hotel.

What would have happened, she wondered grimly as she carefully crossed the street, if she had stayed in Lightning Ridge and come back as originally planned?

Gemma shuddered to think that she would have innocently gone back home to her husband's bed, unknowing of his treachery, unsuspecting of how callously he had betrayed her over the weekend, how he would go on betraying her.

Innocent.

Unknowing.

Unsuspecting.

Well, she wasn't innocent any longer and she would never be unknowing or unsuspecting again. From this moment on, Gemma Whitmore would place her trust in one person only.

Herself.

CHAPTER THREE

CELESTE surveyed her wardrobe with some concern on the Monday morning, moving outfit after outfit along the racks in her dressing-room, mulling over the effect each one would have on Byron Whitmore. What could she wear that wouldn't inspire contempt in his eyes?

Or lust.

At this last thought, Celeste brought herself up sharply. What on earth was the matter with her, caring what Byron thought, or felt? It was her own feelings she had to worry about. Her own lust. Or desire. Or whatever people called it these days.

She'd read somewhere recently that lust had a chemical basis, hormones or such sparking off endorphins in the brain which in turn impelled one's body to mate with the object of its desire without any reference to logic or common sense. A mindless animal thing, in other words.

A mindless animal thing was all she could possibly still feel for that man, she'd decided bitterly after her run-in with Damian at the weekend. Nothing else. Certainly not anything finer or deeper. She'd been silly even to consider such a possibility, let alone worry about it!

Since this was the case, she reasoned ruthlessly, then the person who needed protecting was *herself*, not Byron. How better to protect herself than to dress as provocatively as she always had, thereby ensuring his lust *and* contempt?

Celeste knew full well that the holier-than-thou Byron Whitmore would not contaminate himself by touching someone who epitomised everything he despised. She was safe, as long as she ran true to form. Whereas if she came out looking unexpectedly demure, shock might make him

vulnerable to the primitive desires she knew still lurked
in that staunchly high-principled soul of his. She'd seen
the lust in his eyes the night of the ball as surely as she
had felt her own.

A canary-yellow dress jumped out at her and she drew
it from the rack, smiling. If that didn't put some fire in
his veins and disgust into those beautiful blue eyes of his
then her name wasn't Celeste Campbell.

Made of stretch jersey wool, the yellow sheath fitted
her like a glove and finished mid-thigh. The high rolled
neck and long tight sleeves practised reverse physiology
by being more provocative than the lowest-cut, most revealing style. Perhaps this had something to do with the
way it clung, projecting a subtle promise rather than
overt promiscuity.

Subtle?

Celeste laughed. There was nothing subtle about that
yellow dress if it was worn without a bra and only tights
underneath—the ones with built-in panties which had not
a single ridge to reveal their existence. She had worn it
that way to the races one day and caused a minor sensa-
tion. Celeste remembered the occasion with wry affec-
tion because her photograph had been splashed across all
the Sunday society pages and she felt confident Byron
would have seen them. There was nothing that made her
feel better than the knowledge she might have upset
Byron's equilibrium.

It was not simply a matter of a woman scorned having
her revenge, as her brother probably believed. It was a
matter of justice. Byron had to be punished for what he
had set in motion with his merciless ambition. She
shouldn't have to be the only one to suffer.

The image of her lovely little baby girl swam before her
eyes for a moment before she ruthlessly forced it down,
down into the depths of darkness, hopefully never to
surface again. She'd trained herself not to think about
that any more, for what was the point? She'd done all
that she could, had tried to find her baby. Tried and tried
and tried. In the end, she had had to put the search side

and go on with her life. Either that, or kill herself, or go mad.

Her decision to put the past behind her and go on living had been a brave one. Of course, that didn't mean she no longer suffered, or that she was totally successful in blocking those crippling memories. This was the second time this year she had lapsed. The first time had been when she'd seen that damned opal. How could she *not* have started thinking about the past when confronted by a piece of it? But confronting an inanimate object was nothing compared to confronting the man who'd set all the horrors in motion.

Celeste shuddered, then stiffened and straightened, using every ounce of her iron will to smooth the pained anguish from her face. Her tiger's eyes, which had mirrored intense distress for a second, now flashed with the type of coldly glittering lights that would have terrified any enemy.

Celeste only had one enemy within reach these days. Byron Whitmore.

If I wear the matching yellow sandals complete with three-inch heels, she decided with icy determination, I should meet him eye to eye.

Well, not quite, she conceded drily as she draped the yellow dress over her arm and picked up those same yellow sandals. Byron stretched the tape measure to six feet four. If that wasn't daunting enough, he had shoulders like axe-handles and legs any football player would kill for. Top that off with a classically handsome face which was ageing better than Cary Grant's and you had a man so damned attractive it was downright unfair!

What irked Celeste as well was that Byron's sex appeal was not dimmed by his possessing the sort of chauvinistic attitude to women that sent feminists into a right flap. Yet, for some weird and wonderful reason, most women responded to his strongly male stance very positively. They became coy in his presence. Coy and fluttering and feminine. She herself had been guilty of such a reaction in the old days, as had dear sweet Irene. Oh, yes, Irene had been putty in his hands, quite the reverse of the

hard-edged sarcastic bitch everyone else had known her
to be.

Thinking about the way she herself had blindly responded to Byron in the past rehardened Celeste's heart
towards him in the present. Unfortunately, her emotional toughness did not seem to spill over into other
areas. Her mind and body were running their own races,
recalling things she would rather not recall.

Byron, kissing her in his office when she'd been only
seventeen.

Byron, making love to her. Once again in his office.

Byron, making love to her yet again. Not in his office.
On the billiard-table. At Belleview. Two years later...

For a few tormenting moments she could almost feel
how it had felt when he made love to her. God, she would
have done anything he wanted. She *had* done anything he
wanted!

Celeste squeezed her eyes tightly shut, detesting herself for the wave of heat flooding her body. But when her
nipples actually hardened, her eyes flung open wide in
shock.

Furious with herself for her lack of control, Celeste
swept back into her luxurious bedroom, dumping her
clothes on the huge round bed before heading for her
equally luxurious bathroom. Arousal quickly gave way
to other more satisfying emotions, a vengeful smile
curving her generous mouth as she slipped the silky robe
from her shoulders and snapped on the shower taps.
God, but she was going to enjoy making that bastard's
loins itch today. It was the least she could do in the face
of her own damnable desires.

CELESTE'S BITTER RESOLVE lasted right up till the moment her taxi pulled up in front of the court-house and
she saw Byron walking down the street towards her. Her
immediate flutter of nerves mocked her determination to
be ruthlessly seductive in his presence, her instantly
churning stomach bringing with it both irritation and
dismay.

What in God's name was the matter with her? This was
Byron Whitmore here, the man who'd almost destroyed
her. No mercy, Celeste. No mercy!

Damn, but he did look good in that black suit. Distinguished and handsome, yet incredibly sexy. She couldn't take her eyes off him.

The driver curtly announcing the fare snapped Celeste out of her emotional confusion. She handed him over a note, told him brusquely to keep the change, then began to alight from the back seat, just as Byron drew alongside. Their eyes met as she swung the door wide and presented her long legs to the spring sunshine.

Byron halted mid-stride to glare at her, his blue eyes soothingly derisive as they raked over her, taking in everything she'd wanted him to take in. This was familiar ground to Celeste and she indulged in a smug smile. With her self-confidence restored, she uncurled her tall athletic body with the sensuous grace of a Siamese cat, swinging the door shut behind her before turning to face her foe.

'Good morning, Byron,' she said huskily, that confidently sensual smile firmly in place.

Byron seemed to stiffen under its impact, which only made her sense of satisfaction increase. She revelled in the way his eyes followed her every movement as she smoothed the tight skirt down over her hips, then adjusted the brim of her wide straw hat.

'For God's sake, Celeste,' he snapped at last, blue eyes glittering. 'You're going to a trial, not the races.'

So! He *had* seen those photos of her in the paper. *Good.*

'Looking at you,' she returned silkily while she idly played with the gold rope necklace hanging between her breasts, 'one might have thought we were off to a funeral. Truly, Byron, you should never wear black. Grey's your colour. And you shouldn't scowl like that. It's bad for your health. Gives you high blood-pressure. A man your age has to worry about such things.'

The muscles in Byron's jaw convulsed as though he was clenching and unclenching his teeth. He seemed to be doing the same with his hands. His eyes, however, kept flicking back to her chest where she could feel her braless nipples growing more erect by the moment. Far from being disconcerted by this as she had been earlier on, Celeste found that her own arousal fuelled her to be even more outrageous.

'Did you know that owning a pet can lower your blood-pressure?' she purred. 'It has something to do with the stroking. You look like you could do with a pet, Byron. Not a dog, though. A cat. A nice soft sensual cat that enjoys a lot of stroking...'

Their eyes locked, Celeste lifting a saucy eyebrow at him while she awaited Byron's reaction to her provocative words.

Those beautiful blue eyes of his blazed for a second before they turned icily contemptuous. Celeste smiled her satisfaction with the way the encounter was going. Byron was so predictable.

'Thank you for the advice, Celeste,' he bit out, 'but I think I know what clothes suit me after all these years. As for my blood-pressure,' he went on drily, 'it's just fine. I have no need of a cat, nor any other artificial method of relaxation.'

'Really?' Her smile was a deliciously sarcastic curve. 'Oh, I *see*! Silly me. I did hear you were getting married again. I forgot. Yes, you're right, there's nothing to compare with mother nature's natural relaxant, is there?'

Byron's frozen stare unnerved Celeste for a moment.

'I am not getting married again,' he said coldly.

Celeste thought she hid her reaction very well. 'You're not?' she said airily. 'Well, there you are. People say you should only believe half of what you see and none of what you hear.'

'Where you're concerned, Celeste,' he returned frostily, 'I believe everything I see and add considerably to all that I hear.'

Her laughter was light and flirtatious. 'You're such a flatterer! Shouldn't we be going inside?'

Without waiting for his reply, she turned and began walking up the never-ending steps. He automatically fell into step beside her, Celeste suddenly finding his nearness claustrophobic, which was rather perverse. Hadn't she wanted to tease him, to inflame his unrequited desire for her?

'You came in a taxi,' he remarked on the way up. 'What happened to your Rolls?'

'Nothing. It's in the garage at home. It's simply minus one chauffeur.'

Byron slanted her a sardonic glance. 'What happened? Didn't he come up to expectations?'

'Obviously not. Didn't your fiancée?'

Byron ground to a halt. 'Catherine was never my fiancée.'

'Oh? What was she, then?' Celeste was unnerved by the pleasure she found in the word—*was*.

'A friend.'

'A *close* friend, from all reports. And quite a deal younger than you.'

Byron's handsome face darkened. 'At least she wasn't on my payroll!'

'You think women like that are free?' Celeste countered caustically. 'I'll bet she knew what you were worth, right down to your last dollar. And I'll bet she thought an affair was a down-payment on a more permanent contract.'

'Then she thought wrong.'

Celeste heard the harsh note in his voice. 'What happened, Byron?' she queried softly, moving closer and reaching out to touch him on the wrist. 'Did you find out she was a mercenary gold-digging bitch? You poor darling . . .' Her fingernail slid down his sleeve, over his cuff and onto bare flesh. 'Better to stick to the devil you know in future, don't you think?'

For a few excruciatingly tense seconds, Celeste thought he was actually going to drag her into his arms and kiss her. His eyes were like hot coals on her softly parted lips, his chest rising and falling with visibly unchecked passion.

But Byron did not let her down. He gathered himself superbly, giving her the coldest look while he lifted her hand from the back of his with obvious distaste.

'I'd appreciate it if you would keep your hands to yourself,' he drawled. 'I don't know where they've been.'

Celeste's heart contracted fiercely at this open insult. You'll keep, Byron, she thought savagely. You'll keep.

Outwardly, she delivered a silky smile. 'Shall we adjourn to courtroom six?'

'By all means,' he returned, just as smoothly.

Courtroom six, however, was not where they ended up. Instead, they were shuffled into a waiting-room where there was nothing to do but wait till they were called to the witness stand. The minutes ticked away with endless tedium. Celeste finding it difficult to remain in the same room with Byron without the soothing comfort of his ongoing contempt. A silently brooding Byron was far too attractive to her recently renewed desire for him.

Celeste contemplated starting a conversation about the night of the ball, and the robbery, and what he was going to say in the witness stand. But that would lead to talk about the Heart of Fire. And while she would have liked to question Byron again over how that rotten opal had come to turn up again, she couldn't bear dredging up any more memories today, certainly not *those* memories . . .

'Tell me, what's happening with your family?' she asked Byron so abruptly that he jumped in his seat.

He eyed her suspiciously. 'Why would you want to know about my family?'

Her shrug was nonchalant. 'Why not? They're my family too, in a roundabout sort of way. Besides, I'm fed up with that old feud nonsense between the Whitmores and the Campbells. We should let bygones be bygones.'

'Pardon me if I say I don't believe that for a moment,' he scoffed. 'You singlehandedly revived the old feud when you took over Campbell Jewels. Your mother might have been prepared to let bygones be bygones after your father died. But not, you, Celeste. Never you.'

'A woman can change her mind, can't she?'

Byron laughed. 'You mean you're going to drop all your unfair business tactics? You're not going to deliberately undercut our prices, even at your own expense?

You're not going to bribe any more Japanese tour guides to bypass our stores in favour of yours?'

'That was not done with my sanction,' she said sharply.

'Then I suggest you get rid of your sales and marketing manager before he ruins you.'

'I have spoken to Damian.'

'*Spoken*? He should have been fired!'

'He's family,' she sighed. 'You must know what that's like. I feel responsible for him.'

Celeste was surprised to see understanding soften Byron's face. 'Yes,' he sighed as well. 'I do. But one makes a lot of mistakes in the name of family responsibility.'

Celeste nodded her agreement while Byron fell silent.

'Ava's getting married,' he resumed abruptly after a short interval.

'Good lord!' Celeste was genuinely surprised. 'Who to?'

'A very interesting man by the name of Vince Morelli.'

'An Italian?'

'An Australian-Italian. In his early thirties and handsome as the devil, though not in a typically Latin fashion. He has the colouring and the body of a Bondi lifesaver.'

'Well, I am surprised. I'm afraid I rather saw Ava going to her grave a spinster. Are you sure he's not after her money? As your only sister, she must have quite an inheritance.'

'He has more than enough money of his own. Runs a construction company that specialises in building blocks of units. My solicitor says he's rock-solid.'

She threw him a dry look. 'I see you had him checked out.'

'I didn't get where I am today by being trusting, Celeste. Still, you wouldn't have so many doubts if you saw Ava today. She's trimmed off a lot of weight and is looking positively glowing. Being in love suits her.'

Celeste flinched inside. 'How nice for her,' she said a little stiffly. 'Speaking of being in love, has Jade tied the knot yet with that hunk of a fiancé she was with at the ball?'

'Yes, and she's expecting a baby.'

Celeste had to fight hard this time not to show a thing on her face. 'Really,' she said with a falsely bright smile. 'Is she going to stay home and give up her career?'

'No such luck, Celeste. Kyle's the one who's retiring. Apparently, he fancies himself a house husband while Jade stays head of marketing at Whitmore's.'

'Just my luck,' she muttered. 'But let's not talk about business. What's this I hear about Nathan's marriage being on the rocks?'

'What rubbish!' Byron exclaimed hotly. 'Nathan and Gemma are extremely happy.'

'Well, there, you see what I mean? How can one believe what one hears? Nathan's blissfully happy with his child bride and you're not getting married again, either. I really must stop listening to gossip. Are you sure you're not getting married again? You're not just trying to keep it a secret, are you?'

'I have no intention of ever getting married again,' Byron bit out.

'Oh? Why's that? Wasn't your one experience with marriage a happy one?'

'You know damned well what my marriage was like, Celeste.'

'I'm not sure I do. Why don't you tell me?'

'I am not going to rake over old coals. Neither am I going to speak ill of the dead. Irene tried to be a good wife to me, and I did my best to be a good husband to her.'

'But you didn't love her.'

'Don't you dare talk to me about love,' he snarled. 'You have no concept of what love is.'

Celeste was startled by his sudden vehemence.

'Women like you are poison to all decent men,' he raved on in a low but highly emotional voice. 'You make them think you love them, but you don't. You play games

with them. You turn them inside out. You fuel their desires, use their bodies, and when you've had enough you
throw them away. Well, I called your bluff that last time,
didn't I, Celeste? I used you and I threw you away. Watch
out, darling, or I might do the same thing again. After
all, we both know what you are, don't we? Not a cat. An
alley-cat. I could have you just like that!' And he clicked
his fingers.

It was ironic that at that precise moment Byron was
called to the witness stand. He stood up, and, without a
backward glance, strode proudly from the room.

Celeste stared after him, her heart pounding madly in
her chest. Outrage at his insults warred with the astonishing realisation that Byron might really have loved her
once. Why else would he still be so bitter towards her?
Why else hate her so virulently?

Celeste had always suspected Irene had fed him a whole
lot of lies about her after she'd gone back to school, lies
that had made her look very bad. Even so, Byron had
been very ready to believe those lies, had been very quick
to write her a 'dear John' letter, dismissing their affair as
a temporary infatuation which he deeply regretted. He'd
stated quite coldly that he wanted nothing to do with her
ever again.

Celeste had been crushed by this brutal and rather
confusing rejection, then shattered when a few short
months later he'd married Irene.

Recalling the distress she had felt at that time hardened Celeste's heart again. No, she decided staunchly,
and clenched her teeth down hard in her jaw. Byron's
fierce antagonism towards her just now was no proof of
a past love. He was simply being the same hypocritical
bastard he'd always been, pretending to be holier-than-
thou, judging her on standards that he himself didn't live
up to. He'd lied when he'd told her he loved her back
then. Lied for the sole purpose of possessing her body.
and when he'd had his fill and she'd gone back to school,
he'd callously dumped her and moved on to Irene, who
he'd obviously thought would bring him Campbell

Jewels as well as her beautiful and undoubtedly willing body.

Men like Byron didn't love women, Celeste accepted with a bitter cynicism. They loved sex and money and success. They loved power and position in the community. Nothing was more important to Byron than his social standing, his so-called good name. Why else would he spend so much time and money working for charity? Why else would he have taken that degenerate boy off the streets and adopted him, for heaven's sake?

Because he wanted everyone to look up to him and say what a great man he was. How generous and good. How bloody wonderful!

But that shining reputation of his had been won at a cost. She'd been the one to pay. Yet he had the hide to tear strips off *her* character, as well as the gall to claim he could have her as easily as he could snap his fingers.

Like hell, she thought. Like bloody hell! There was no way she would ever let him touch her again. Never in a million years!

CHAPTER FOUR

GEMMA'S hand trembled as she dialled. It was the hardest thing she had ever had to do but she had to do it. Nathan would be leaving soon to go to the airport to pick her up, and even she didn't have the heart callously to let him worry when she didn't get off that plane.

The telephone in their apartment rang and rang and rang, but he didn't answer. It had not occurred to her that Nathan might not be home, that he might go straight from rehearsals at the theatre to Mascot Airport. But now it did, and she groaned her dismay. God, she just wasn't thinking straight.

With her heart thudding madly in her chest, she hung up hurriedly and looked up the theatre number in the telephone book. This time, someone answered immediately, and luckily Nathan was soon located. He came on the line, sounding worried.

'Gemma? What's wrong, darling? Did you miss the flight?'

'No, Nathan,' she replied, fighting to keep her voice steady. 'I didn't miss the flight.'

'Then where are you ringing from? You're supposed to be in the air. Oh, I see. The flight's been delayed. Never mind, darling. These things happen. So when will you be arriving?'

The two 'darling's had really hurt, bringing the sense of outrage she needed. 'I won't be arriving, Nathan. I'm not coming home.'

'Not coming home?' he repeated in a stunned, almost blank tone.

'That's right. You told me once that if I ever wanted out of our marriage I was to say so up-front.' She paused long enough to drag in a much needed breath. 'I want out of our marriage, Nathan. My solicitor will be in touch.'

'Wait!' he cried, seemingly aware that she was about to hang up. 'You...you can't just leave me like this, Gemma. You must give me a reason. God-dammit, I have a right to know the reason!' he demanded, clearly shaken.

'The reason? The reason is you're a cheat and a liar. I'm sure it won't take too much intelligence to work out what I'm talking about. You took me for a fool, Nathan. And I'm not. I'm not...' Her voice broke and she struggled for control. 'Oh, God, how could you? I didn't deserve that. I...I...' She broke off and forcibly pulled herself together. 'Goodbye, Nathan. Don't bother trotting out to Lightning Ridge to find me. I'm not there.'

She hung up, then sank down on the side of the hotel bed, looking and feeling utterly drained. No tears came. She was all out of tears.

But dear God, whatever was she going to do? Where was she going to go?

Her overnight stay in the old hotel and many hours of thinking had provided no solutions except that she was going to divorce Nathan. No doubt some fancy solicitor could drive a hard bargain for her when it came to a financial settlement, but she automatically shrank from that and from what people would say about her. They'd only been married a few months, after all. She also shrank from having to tell Nathan's family the reason for her leaving him—that he'd been cheating on her with his ex-wife.

Not that they would necessarily believe her. Nathan would deny it, of course, and so would Lenore. Byron, Gemma realised, would be loath to believe such a thing of his golden-haired boy. Nathan could do no wrong in his eyes, being supposedly as old-fashioned in his moral principles as his adopted father. Ava was the only person Gemma could think of who would be on her side, but how could she put brother against sister? It wasn't right.

No, she would have to strike out on her own. She still had the money Byron had paid her as a reward for bringing back the Heart of Fire. That would cover her expenses for a while. And she could probably get a job easily enough with her mastery of oral Japanese.

Going back to work at Whitmore's was not an option. Even if Byron didn't fire her, Nathan would descend upon her there like an avenging angel, demanding further explanations when doing his best to whitewash his behaviour. He might even throw himself on her mercy and beg her forgiveness. She could not have borne that.

What she needed, more than anything, was to disappear for a while, out of reach of Nathan and any private detective he might hire to find her. Which meant not staying in any hotel, nor going to real estate agents nor applying for a job. That would leave a trail any decent detective would easily pick up on.

So where could she go?

Damian's offer, which had been hovering at the back of her mind all along, but which she had previously dismissed, jumped to the fore. Why not? she rationalised. He was in a position to help her. He had the money and the connections. He'd even promised her a job if she ever wanted one. Campbell Jewels had stores in other states. Maybe she could move to Brisbane or to Melbourne: get herself well away from Sydney and Nathan.

At three in the afternoon, Damian would probably be in his office. Gemma looked up the number of the head office of Campbell Jewels and, once again, dialled.

'Could I speak to Damian Campbell, please?' she requested of the girl who answered.

An extension was tried but no one answered.

'Mr Campbell doesn't seem to be in his office at the moment,' the receptionist said with brisk politeness. 'Would you like to leave a message and I'll get him to ring you back?'

Gemma sighed. 'Yes, all right.' And she relayed her name and the hotel number, adding that this was an emergency and she would appreciate every effort being made to get the message to Mr Campbell as soon as possible.

After she had hung up yet again, Gemma lay down in the dimly lit room and closed her eyes. Depression descended, as did exhaustion. She hadn't slept much the previous night. Now, she could not stop her mind from slipping into the blackness.

CELESTE LEFT the court-house in a highly agitated state. Her encounter with Byron was bad enough, but having to face that pig who had manhandled her so brutally the night of the robbery had upset her more than she'd thought it would. Still, she was sure he'd be put behind bars after her solid and unwavering testimony. Men who perpetrated violence against women should be incarcerated and the key thrown away, in her opinion.

She chose to walk back to the office. It was only a couple of blocks and the fresh air would do her mood good. On the way she made a brief stopover in a coffee lounge where she banished some hunger pangs with a roll and some coffee. By the time the lift carried her up to the tenth floor of the city office block that housed the head office of Campbell Jewels, Celeste felt much better.

Five minutes later she was seated behind her large modern desk, reading the monthly sales reports and chewing thoughtfully on a Biro. Shaking her head, she picked up her telephone and asked for Damian's extension, only to be told by his secretary that he wasn't back yet from lunch.

Striding out to Reception, she informed the startled receptionist that Mr Campbell was to be sent into her office the moment he reappeared, and not a second later. She was fuming by the time he walked in—without knocking—at five to four.

'You wanted to see me, Celeste?' he said with arrogant nonchalance, plonking himself down on the black leather chesterfield and drawing a packet of cigarettes from his pocket.

'I don't allow smoking in here, Damian,' she said coldly.

'Tough. If you don't like it, fire me.' And he lit up, drawing in deeply, then exhaling in her direction.

She glared at him through the haze of smoke. 'I just might do that.'

'No, you won't. Darling Mama holds the ultimate reins in this place and she wouldn't hear of it.'

'Darling Mama is in Europe for another few months,' came Celeste's dry reminder. 'Before she left, she gave me a free hand to do whatever I thought was best for the company. Not in one's wildest imagination could your performance as sales and marketing manager be labelled that. Our retail outlets are still suffering a backlash from the publicity we received over the tour-guide scandal. Our exports are down nearly twenty per cent. And the quality of the opals we've been using leaves a lot to be desired.'

'Shocking,' he murmured, clearly not at all concerned.

Celeste's eyes narrowed on him. 'Have you been drinking, Damian?'

His smirk was revealing. 'I may have had a tipple or two with lunch. Is that against the rules as well?'

'No. But having a three-hour lunch is. You were supposed to be back at your desk at two. It's after four.'

'Is it really?' he mocked. 'I must have lost track of time.'

'Damian,' she said sternly. 'You must realise I can't allow this to go on.'

'Why not? The family's so rich that Campbell Jewels could go bankrupt and we'd still be all right. Your obsession with trying to outdo Whitmore Opals all the time is such a bore and so unnecessary. You should be out there enjoying yourself, like I do.'

'Doing what?' she snapped. 'Drinking yourself silly and playing poker?'

'Tch tch. Such spleen. I take it your meeting with Mr Whitmore in court did not go to your liking? What went wrong? Didn't he succumb to the charms you so discreetly put on display today?' His black gaze encompassed her thoroughly, noting her high colour as well as her figure-hugging clothing.

'You don't know what you're talking about, Damian. And you're trying to change the subject.'

'Is that what I'm doing? I thought I was sitting here, smoking.'

'You really are quite drunk, aren't you?'

'Uh-huh.'

'That's it then. As of today, you're no longer the sales and marketing manager. I won't sack you completely. I wouldn't do that to Mother. But I'm moving you into some useless position where you can't do any harm. You can be director of public relations.'

'Director of public relations? We haven't *got* a director of public relations!'

'Exactly. It should be right up your alley. No one will notice or care if you came to work or not.'

Celeste watched Damian's annoyance disappearing as the practicality of his new position sank in. 'Sounds perfect,' he drawled. 'And who are you going to get to replace me?'

She made a dismissive gesture with the Biro. 'I'm sure there must be someone in this company who can do the job.'

Damian laughed. 'I'm sure there is. I can see him now. He'll be bright and young and handsome, not to mention prepared to be extremely grateful to the boss.'

Celeste had had just about enough. 'Damian, I'm warning you. I—'

A sharp tap on the door stopped her in mid-flow.

'Come in,' she said sharply, knowing her assistant would not interrupt like this unless it was very important.'

'Yes, Luke?' she asked when he popped his head in the door.

'Miss Landers says an urgent message came in for Mr Campbell a while back, but she only just found out he *had* returned from lunch and was in here.'

'What is it?' Damian asked, swivelling round.

'Here... She wrote down the name and number.' He handed over a piece of paper to Damian, who remained seated where he was. 'The lady said it was an emergency

and you were to ring her back as soon as you came in.'
Luke nodded towards Celeste, then left, shutting the door
with discreet quiet behind him.

Celeste was shocked by the look of sly glee that came
into Damian's eyes as he read the note. 'Fantastic,' he
muttered, then jumped to his feet. 'I must go.'

'Wait a minute, Damian! Who is this woman? And
what's the emergency?'

'That, my dear sister,' he said with dark passion in his
voice, 'is none of your business.'

'I hope you're not getting tangled up with another
married woman.'

He threw her a scornful look. 'I never get *tangled up*
with a married woman, Celeste.'

'That's just playing with words. You know what I
meant.'

'Yes, of course I do. And as I said before, mind your
own damned business!'

There was nothing quiet or discreet about Damian's
exit. He slammed the door after him, leaving Celeste
feeling more worried about her brother than she'd been
in years. Drinking. Gambling. Getting into debt. Having affairs with other men's wives. Where would it all
end?

She shook her head and looked back down at the appalling sales reports. There was nothing she could do
about Damian, but there was something she could do
about Campbell's dwindling profits. Reaching over, she
pressed the intercom button.

'Yes, Ms Campbell?' Luke answered.

'I need to see you,' she rapped out. 'Straight away.'

'Coming...'

Luke presented himself immediately, adjusting his tie
a little self-consciously as he came to attention in front of
her desk. At thirty, he was older than her previous assistant, and not nearly as handsome. But he knew how to
dress to make the most of his very good body and he
knew how to follow orders. Above all, he was intelligent
and ambitious. Ruthlessly so, she believed. Every now
and then, a cool sharpness came into those bland grey

eyes of his, giving him a totally different look. Celeste sometimes wondered what he would have done if her occasional public flirtation with him had been put to the acid test. To be honest, she had a feeling he would have turned her down, which was perhaps why she was about to give him the chance of a lifetime.

'As of this moment, Luke,' she said crisply, 'the position of sales and marketing manager is vacant. Mr Campbell is going to take over a new position in the company as director of public relations. I was wondering if you'd be interested in his old position.'

Celeste was gratified with Luke's reaction. He was suitably stunned for a split-second, but quickly assumed that cool and highly self-contained bearing she rather admired.

'I would indeed,' was all he said. There was no gushing, no grovelling.

Celeste smiled at him. Yes, she thought with great satisfaction. You'll do. You'll do splendidly.

CHAPTER FIVE

GEMMA was wrenched out of a deep sleep by someone shaking her. Her eyes sprang open to find Damian Campbell sitting on the hotel bed beside her, peering worriedly down into her face. There was another equally worried-looking man hovering behind him. It took her a few moments to recognise him as the desk clerk from downstairs.

'Are you all right, Gemma?' Damian was asking anxiously. 'You haven't done anything silly, have you?'

'Wh...what?' she stammered, her head still fuzzy from sleep. 'I...I...don't know what you mean.'

Damian smiled. 'She's fine,' he threw over his shoulder at the desk clerk. 'You can go now. Thanks for letting me in. False alarm.'

Gemma's mind slowly started working. She levered herself up on one elbow and watched the man leave. When he'd closed the door, her gaze returned to Damian. 'What on earth did you tell him? My God, you thought I might have tried to kill myself, didn't you?'

Damian shrugged. 'Who knows what you might have done? I didn't get your message for quite a while and you did say it was an emergency. When I rang the number and found out it was a hotel not far from the city, I decided to hot-foot it right over here instead of just ringing. Then when I knocked on your door, you didn't answer.'

'I was *asleep*!'

'I can see that now.'

His smile was so sweet, Gemma couldn't stay angry with him. 'I...I've left Nathan,' she admitted unhappily, swinging her feet over the side of the bed and sitting up properly.

'I gathered that,' came Damian's gentle reply. He picked up her closest hand, stroking it soothingly with his other hand. After an initial instinctive resistance, Gemma soon found the action both relaxing and comforting. She closed her eyes and sighed.

'I always knew it was just a matter of time,' Damian said.

A sob caught in Gemma's throat. Damian dropped her hand to put one arm around her shoulder, the other stroking her head as he cradled it against his chest. Once again, she did not have the strength to resist him, and it did feel good to be held so tenderly.

'Poor darling,' he crooned. 'I can just imagine what it was like, married to that bastard. You did the right thing, leaving him before it was too late.'

'Maybe it is too late,' she muttered miserably. Gemma knew in her heart that she would never love another man. Nathan had vowed to make her his and she *was*, with every fibre of her being. Maybe that was why she felt so lost and so lonely. Because the very essence of her life had been taken from her.

Suddenly, and for the umpteenth time, she started to cry. Damian let her till the last sobs hiccuped their way to nothing. It was then that he made his suggestion, a suggestion she was too emotionally drained to turn down. She was only too glad to have somewhere to go, and someone to take her there.

CELESTE HAD to take a taxi home from work, for what else could she do? Damian had not returned to work after an apparently dramatic exit from his office, so he wasn't there to give her a lift home. She no longer had a chauffeur to take her everywhere in the Rolls and did not feel inclined to hire another. Yet she did not drive herself. She did actually have a licence, but when circumstances had prevented her driving for a number of years she had somehow never found the nerve to get behind the wheel again. Odd, really, when she had found the nerve to do plenty of other things.

With a sigh, she settled into the back seat of the taxi and prepared herself mentally for a hair-raising trip home. That was the one thing she deplored about taxis. The drivers! Thank the lord she didn't live far from the city.

The heavy traffic went some way to stopping the trip from reducing her to a nervous wreck, but she was still glad when the cab turned down her street.

Campbell Court—as the family home was called—had a very exclusive address in Point Piper, right at the end of a cool leafy street that ran along the shores of Sydney Harbour. The huge granite manor-style house stood grandly on a rise at the front of the large block amid superb grounds, rolling lawns sloping down behind the house, first to a terrace where the pool-house sat, then down to the waterline and a private jetty. Moored not far out from this jetty was the yacht which Celeste had personally inherited on her father's death.

It was called the *Celeste*, and Stewart Campbell had brought it for a song in the fifties, but it was now conservatively worth six million dollars and needed a crew of ten to man it. Celeste rarely, if ever, took it out, choosing to use it as an exclusive setting for business luncheons and dinner parties. It was a good getaway spot as well, especially when her mother was in residence at Campbell Court and was having one of her infernal musical soirées, full of pretentious people.

Much as she loved her mother—who really was a softie despite being a social snob—Celeste was always glad when her remaining parent went away on holiday. Perhaps it was the fact that her mother knew all her dark secrets that sometimes made Celeste ill at ease in her presence.

Not that Adele would ever betray her. She had never breathed an indiscreet word in all these years. But sometimes Celeste would catch her mother looking at her in a certain way, a sad understanding in her eyes. Invariably this was when Celeste was being outrageous, or ruthlessly tough, and Celeste would suddenly want to scream at her, It's not my fault. Can't you see? I have to be this way. It's how I survive!

Celeste's train of thought was broken when she spied a navy blue Mercedes in the driveway of her home, parked in front of the security gates. She didn't recognise the car. Who could it belong to? There was someone sitting behind the wheel, but it was getting dark at six-thirty and she couldn't even make out if it was a man or a woman.

'Pull in behind that car, would you?' she directed the taxi driver. He did so and as she paid him Celeste was stunned to see Nathan Whitmore alighting from the Mercedes.

'What on earth is he doing here?' she muttered under her breath, frowning as she herself climbed out of the taxi and swung the door shut. The taxi immediately accelerated away, leaving Celeste to walk over to where Nathan had remained standing beside his car.

Those cold grey eyes of his swept over her as she approached and Celeste found herself bristling.

There was something about Byron's adopted son that had always irritated her. He was too everything. Too handsome. Too smooth. Too controlled.

Not that she'd had much to do with him over the years. She'd run into him occasionally at various social functions, and found that, even from a distance, he could present a disturbing figure. He could look across the room at you without any visible expression on his face, but you would still want to shiver in your boots.

That was why she'd been taken aback at the ball when he'd almost lost his temper with her. It had been so unlike him. She'd also been taken back by his lovely young bride, whose air of virginal innocence seemed at odds with Nathan's man-of-the-world sophistication. Damian, for one, hadn't been able to take his eyes off her all that night. It had worried Celeste at the time that her brother might pursue the girl, especially when he'd remarked the following day that he'd heard the new Mrs Whitmore wasn't all that happy.

Celeste experienced a sudden awful feeling that she knew why Nathan was on her doorstep.

'Hello, Nathan,' she said crisply. 'To what do I owe this highly unexpected visit?'

He didn't answer her directly, his darkly puzzled frown as bewildering as his reply. 'So you really *weren't* home.'

'Pardon?'

'I was speaking to your housekeeper a while back on phone,' he went on agitatedly, 'and she told me no one was there except herself. I didn't believe her.'

Celeste blinked a couple of times. 'Would you mind telling me what you're talking about?'

He shook his head, the action flopping a wayward blond lock over his high forehead. He immediately raked it back with splayed fingers, shocking Celeste when she saw his hand was actually shaking.

'Gemma hasn't been in touch with you?' he asked, only adding to her confusion.

'Why would your wife be in touch with *me*?'

He stared into her face as though trying to see if she was lying. His steely grey eyes narrowed, and she just stopped herself from shivering. Men like Nathan always frightened her a little. They were so secretive, both with their thoughts and their actions, which they never explained. She hated that.

'If you've nothing else to add, Nathan,' she said curtly, 'it's been a long day, I'm tired and I would like to go inside.'

His hand shot out to enclose her arm. 'You swear to me that Gemma has not contacted you today, either in person or by telephone?'

'Take . . . your . . . hand . . . off . . . my . . . arm,' she enunciated very slowly and very clearly.

Perhaps Nathan recalled what had happened to that creep who had manhandled her at the ball. Whatever, his hand slipped from her arm and Celeste began to breathe again. Nathan didn't know how close he'd come to a karate chop to the neck.

'Well?' he prompted.

'I already told you. Your wife has not been in touch with me. What in God's name makes you think she would have been? We hardly know each other. In fact, we *don't* know each other. You're not making any sense.'

'Nothing makes sense now,' he muttered.

When his shoulders sagged, he looked so dejected and wretched that Celeste felt an unexpected sympathy for him. Damn, she hoped Damian had nothing to do with this. It was clear as the nose on her face that Nathan's wife had left him. It was also too much of a coincidence that Damian had received an urgent message from some lady-friend this afternoon and gone racing to her rescue like a knight in shining armour. Only Damian was no white knight. He was the devil incarnate when it came to sweet young things like Gemma Whitmore.

But there was no way she was going to relay any of these suspicions to Nathan. God knows what he might do if she said his wife might be with her brother.

'Am I to assume your wife has left you?' Celeste asked.

His steely grey eyes projected the most peculiar hate her way. 'If she has, I know who to thank for it.'

'My God, you're crazy, do you know that? I had nothing to do with any of this!'

He glared at her, before making a frustrated sound and shaking his head in a disconsolate fashion. 'If that wasn't what she meant, then what *did* she mean?'

Celeste was getting angry with his totally cryptic remarks. 'Nathan, I'm sorry, but I can't help you with this. It's none of my business.'

It *is* none of my business, Celeste kept telling herself. I don't want to get mixed up in any of it. Nathan means nothing to me and neither does his wife. Let them sort their own lives out.

So why was it that, when Nathan climbed into his car and drove away, she was left feeling hopelessly agitated? Was it that she suspected Damian had played a role in the break-up? That didn't make much sense. Damian had played a role in the break-up of several marriages and while she didn't condone his behaviour—was, in fact, disgusted with his morals—she hadn't been personally affected by any of his tacky affairs.

This time, however, she couldn't get Nathan Whitmore out of her mind. Or was it that lovely young wife of his she couldn't stop thinking about? Celeste was appalled to think Damian had spirited her away somewhere and might be, at this very moment, seducing her.

My God, she suddenly realised. Maybe they were inside Campbell Court! She hadn't thought of that.

Celeste hurried over to the small side security gate, using her key to let herself in then striding forth up the paved driveway to the house.

'Cora?' she called out to the housekeeper as she let herself in. 'Cora, where are you?'

'Back here, Celeste,' came the reply from the direction of the kitchen.

Celeste tossed her straw hat on to the hat stand in the corner of the entrance hall before striding down the black and white tiled hall, glancing in the various living-rooms as she went. They were empty.

'Is Damian home?' she asked on entering the kitchen.

Cora looked up from where she was doing the vegetables. A plain spare woman in her fifties, she was as sharp as a tack when it came to the family she'd been the housekeeper for for more than a decade. A widow, she lived in during the week, staying with her married sister at the weekends. Her shrewd gaze took in Celeste's agitation at once.

'No, he's not,' she said, then added exasperatedly, 'What's he been up to this time?'

'God only knows.' Celeste sagged on to a kitchen stool. 'Has he rung?'

'No.'

'Damn.' She bit her lip and wondered where he could possibly be. She had suspected for a while that he had a flat somewhere where he took women. Either that, or he had dubious friends who let him use their places for romantic rendezvous. Of course, they could also be holed up in some hotel or motel somewhere, assuming they were together. She *was* just assuming this, after all. Maybe Damian wasn't involved.

It was a slim hope and one she clung to for all of ten seconds.

'What am I going to do with him, Cora?' she muttered dispiritedly.

'There's nothing you can do, Celeste. He's ruined.'

Celeste squeezed her eyes shut while her heart flip-flopped. 'Yes, you're right. He is ruined. Totally. So why do I still care about him?'

'Why does any of us care about him? Because we love him, I suppose, no matter what he is or what he's done. He does have some good qualities, you know.'

'Name one.'

Cora was clearly at a loss, but Celeste knew what she meant. Damian had a way with women in general, not just the ones he wanted to seduce. He remembered things like birthdays and anniversaries. And he seemed to know just what to say sometimes to make you feel special. No doubt it was mostly only manipulative flattery and clever conning, but it worked.

'The problem is,' Celeste went on sadly, 'he's ruining other people's lives as well. He has to be stopped.'

'How?'

She shook her head, her heart heavy. 'I don't know.'

Both women fell silent, and it was into this depressed silence that the telephone rang.

'Maybe that's him now,' Cora suggested. 'He's usually fairly thoughtful when it comes to telling me if he's not going to be home for dinner.'

Nerves fluttered in Celeste's stomach as she made her way back to where an extension rested on a table in the front hall. If it was Damian, what could she possibly say to him? He'd already told her to mind her own business back in her office.

'Campbell Court,' she answered, trying to stay cool.

'It's Damian, Celeste. Just ringing to let Cora know I won't be home for dinner.'

'Oh? Aren't you coming home at all?'

'No.'

'Where are you staying, then?'

'With a friend.'

Celeste swallowed then decided to take the plunge. 'Damian, are you with Gemma Whitmore?'

There was no doubting his sharp intake of breath.

'Please don't lie to me,' she raced on. 'Nathan Whitmore was waiting here when I got home.'

'*Nathan*? At *Campbell Court*?'

Celeste could hear a female make a frightened gasping sound in the background. Who else but Nathan's wife would react like that to the sound of his name?

'Hold on there a moment, Celeste.'

There was some kind of muffled interchange before Damian came back on the line.

'What did Nathan want?' he asked.

'He didn't really say. He didn't make much sense. I don't think he was himself. She is there with you, Damian, isn't she?'

'Yes.'

Celeste closed her eyes for a second on a silent groan. 'Have you been having an affair with her, Damian?' she asked, trying to keep the weary exasperation out of her voice.

'No,' he denied sulkily. 'I bloody well haven't.'

'Then why did she come to you?'

'She didn't know anybody else in Sydney.'

'What happened, then, to make her leave Nathan? He seemed genuinely perplexed about it all.'

'I have no doubt. He thought he was safe with Gemma out at Lightning Ridge.'

Celeste let out a frustrated sigh. 'Not you, too. Please try to make sense. What on earth has Lightning Ridge got to do with anything?' It vaguely crossed Celeste's mind that this was the second time Lightning Ridge had come into her life lately. Firstly, the Heart of Fire was supposed to have turned up again in Lightning Ridge, and now this. No doubt it would pop up again a third time, since things did seem to happen in threes.

'That's where Gemma grew up,' Damian informed her. 'She'd gone back for a visit and while she was away Nathan spent the weekend with Lenore. Gemma came back unexpectedly early and caught them together.'

Celeste contained her shock while she got the facts. 'Now wait a minute till I get this straight. If Gemma caught Nathan and his ex-wife together then why is he so confused over why she left him?'

'Because Gemma didn't make her presence known. She left without them seeing her.'

'I see . . .'

'She doesn't want to see him or talk to him ever again. She says he knows in his heart why she left him.'

'He was very upset.'

'Tough. So's Gemma.'

Celeste frowned. 'What is she to you, Damian?'

'Butt out, Celeste.'

'If you hurt her, you'll have me to answer to.'

There was dead silence on the other end.

'I want to speak to her,' Celeste demanded.

'No. She's too upset to talk.'

'Bring her home here, then, where she can be properly looked after.'

'Are you serious?'

'Yes, I am.' At least here at Campbell Court, she could keep an eye on things, could perhaps drop a few words of gentle warning about Damian.

'I'll think about it.'

'She'd be safe here,' Celeste argued with quiet logic. 'Nathan probably wouldn't think of looking here again, but we have good security if he does.'

'Yes...yes, I didn't think of that. Nathan's the sort of man who won't let go easily. But Gemma's too tired to go anywhere else tonight. The poor darling's wrung out. I'll bring her there tomorrow.'

'I think that would be wise.'

'Do you just? Goodbye, Celeste,' he said brusquely. 'I'll see you tomorrow some time.'

He hung up, leaving Celeste to stare down into the dead receiver. Damian's manner puzzled her. He sounded as if he was genuinely fond of the girl. Could it be that he had finally fallen in love? *Really* in love?

   If he had, it would be the first time that she knew of.
The only person Damian had previously been in love with
had been himself.

   Her thoughts turned to Nathan and his affair with his
ex-wife. Much as she didn't like the man, this news had
shocked her. He'd only been married for a few months,
after all. Not that she should be surprised by the things
men did when in the grip of lust.

   Still, it was perfectly clear to Celeste that Nathan had
no idea his wife was *au fait* with his adultery. Perhaps if
he knew the reason why she'd left him then he'd let her
go quietly, without any fuss. It worried Celeste that violence might erupt between Nathan and Damian, if and
when he found out who Gemma was with. Men were violent creatures. That, she was sure of.

   Telephoning Nathan directly was out of the question.
He would quite rightly jump to the conclusion that his
wife was with Damian. For how else would Celeste have
gained such information? She wanted him to know
Gemma knew about his being unfaithful, but she didn't
want him to know where Gemma was. Obviously, what
she needed was a go-between ...

   It didn't take Celeste too long to come up with the
perfect person, the *only* person who she could trust to do
the job tactfully and with discretion.

   A rueful smile creased her mouth at her putting words
such as trust and tact in the same sentence as Byron
Whitmore. But her hatred for the man was not a blind
hatred. She knew his good points as well as his bad.

   Telephoning Byron, however, after what had happened today, was not something Celeste was keen about.
In fact, she just couldn't face it on an empty stomach.
What difference would an hour or two make? She would
ring him after dinner, and after several glasses of wine.

   'That was Damian,' she told Cora on re-entering the
kitchen. 'You're right. He won't be home for dinner.' She
headed straight for the refrigerator where she extracted
a bottle of her favourite Chardonnay, then proceeded to
open it. With the cork dumped into the bin, she selected
a good-sized wine glass from the glass cupboard, picked

up the bottle and headed for the door. 'I'm off to shower and change, Cora. I'll eat here with you in the kitchen. You won't mind if I'm in my nightwear, will you?'

'You could go to a ball in your nightwear,' Cora called after her.

Celeste laughed, for she did have a penchant for glamorous lingerie, but the word 'ball' quickly reminded her of Byron and what she had to do after dinner. Groaning, she stopped at the base of the staircase and poured some wine into the glass, gulping it all down before giving a wry chuckle and starting up the stairs. If only some of her business associates could see her now, having to get some Dutch courage out of a bottle.

She paused on the landing halfway up the stairs to have another deep swallow, lifting the glass to the stained-glass window in front of her. 'Here's to you, kid,' she toasted the angel who stared expressionlessly back down at her. 'Not much to say for yourself, have you?' she muttered. 'Still, I guess I'd get a damned shock if you ever did talk back to me. Good grief, I must be going potty talking to a window. Is that one step up from talking to the wall or one step down? See you later, window. I dare say by the time I pass this way again, I'll have sorted out that crucial question. If not, it certainly won't bother me any more.'

Celeste laughed, poured herself another glassful of wine and headed for the shower.

CHAPTER SIX

CELESTE liked the feel of satin against her bare skin. No other material was as cool, or as smooth or as soft. All her nightwear was made of satin, mostly in neutral or smoky colours that looked good at night and flattered her rather delicate colouring. Ivory, oyster, pearl, champagne and a silvery grey, they were her favourite colours. Occasionally, she would wear a dusky blue or pink. Never black. She didn't like to wear black, yet she wasn't sure why. Black looked well against her blonde hair, but she always shied away from it.

The nightie she put on after her shower was a silvery grey, full length and quite simple with a deep V neckline and tiny shoe-string straps. Her arms raised, it slithered down over her freshly washed and powdered skin, the top moulding around her small firm breasts, the rest falling in deep folds to the floor. Slipping her feet into low-heeled fluffy white mules, Celeste drew on the matching robe, which flowed and floated around her as she swanned back down the stairs, pausing briefly to send a mocking glance up at the angel.

'You still there?' she taunted. 'What do you think of this outfit? You don't like satin? Too bad. I do. What about my hair? It looks good caught up at the sides like this, doesn't it?'

Hell, I'm smashed, she thought as she sashayed down the rest of the stairs, still carrying the glass and wine-bottle, though both were now empty.

It had been years since she had drunk a whole bottle of wine—before dinner, that was—and it had really gone to her head. She had to get some food into her before she dissolved down on to the floor somewhere.

Cora, God bless her dear heart, said not a single critical word during the meal, despite Celeste dropping her cutlery, missing her mouth with a forkful of food, at which point she giggled uncontrollably for a while. Despite all this, the alcohol did not dull the distressing awareness that she had to contact the enemy after dinner and tell him something he wasn't going to want to hear.

Celeste went to help clear up afterwards, but the housekeeper waved her away. 'You pay me to do this, Celeste. You go have a swim or something.'

'Straight after dinner?'

'Since when did a little thing like a full stomach stop you going for a swim?' the housekeeper said drily. 'Besides, the exercise might sober you up a bit.'

Celeste laughed. 'What an awful thought. I'll be up in my bedroom if you want me.'

'And I'll be in my room if you want me. There's a movie on television tonight I've been looking forward to seeing.'

'In that case I'll answer the phone if it rings.'

Cora smiled her thanks. 'Everyone should have a boss like you.'

'You're the only one who thinks that, Cora. I'm nicknamed Attila the Hun around the traps.'

'Ah, yes, but they don't know the real you. You're a softie underneath.'

Celeste laughed her way out of the kitchen and along the hall. When she turned to walk up the stairs and encountered the glass-cold eyes of the angel looking down at her, she stopped laughing. 'So what are you turning your nose up at?' she snapped. 'Don't you agree that I'm a softie underneath?'

Lifting up her own nose, she careered back up the stairs and into her bedroom where she flopped her tipsy self down on the bed and reached for the telephone before she lost her nerve. She was actually punching in Byron's number before it occurred to her that she knew his damned number off by heart, yet she hadn't dialled it in donkey's years.

But she'd looked it up plenty of times. Looked it up and stared at it and been tempted to call, call and tell him the awful truth, the crippling truth, the soul-destroying truth. Her courage had always failed her, as it was in danger of doing now. But she persisted, gripping the receiver more tightly with each successive unanswered ring. With a bit of luck, he wouldn't be home.

'Belleview,' Byron answered curtly on the sixth ring.

'It ... it's Celeste here, Byron.'

Dead silence.

Celeste hoped and prayed his reaction was shock that she'd called him at all, and not because she'd sounded as rattled as she was sure she had. Pulling herself together, she continued in a much more controlled manner. 'Sorry to call you at home, or at *all* for that matter, but this was an emergency.'

More silence.

Damn the man! Now she was getting angry. Gritting her teeth, she launched forth again, quite bluntly.

'Nathan's wife has left him.'

'*What* did you say?' Byron stormed down the line so loudly that she flinched and held the receiver away from her ear.

It was a pleasure to keep her cool while he was losing his. 'There's no need to shout, Byron. I can hear you as well as I'm sure you can hear me. And you heard me correctly the first time, I'm sure. Gemma has left Nathan. When I arrived home this evening, he was waiting for me in the driveway, looking for her.'

'And he thought he might find her at *your* place?'

'Believe me, I found it as odd as you do. He seemed pretty upset, I'm afraid, and not thinking straight. I gather he hasn't contacted you about any of this yet?' Celeste had already guessed that he wouldn't have. Men like Nathan solved their own problems, their own way. They didn't run to their fathers for help.

'No, he hasn't,' Byron growled. 'Where is he now, do you know?'

'Probably at home. I told him I couldn't help him and he went away.'

'So why have you rung me? Surely it's not merely to crow, is it? I wouldn't have even taken *you* for being that vicious!'

It irritated Celeste that Byron could still hurt her, but she staunchly ignored the jab of dismay and went on. 'I have since found out some information which you might like to relay to Nathan.'

'What kind of information?'

'When I spoke to him earlier, I gained the impression he had no idea why Gemma had left him. I have since found out the reason.'

'*You* found out the reason?'

'That's right. Gemma made a trip to Lightning Ridge this weekend, didn't she?'

'Yes. She flew there last Friday and was due home today. But what the hell does that have to do with anything? Nathan knew she was going there.'

'I realise that, but the thing is she flew home earlier than expected. When she arrived at wherever she and Nathan live, his ex-wife was there with him in compromising circumstances.'

'Lenore? In bed with Nathan? I don't believe that. I won't believe that.'

'*Don't*, then! But Gemma does and she's the one who's left Nathan. Apparently neither Nathan nor Lenore actually saw her and she simply left.'

'Who told you this? None of this makes sense. Or maybe it does,' he muttered, Celeste almost able to hear his sharp mind ticking over. 'Nathan for some reason thought Gemma would be at Campbell Court... Since she wouldn't be going out there to see *you*, then that only leaves that snake of a brother of yours. Damian's behind all this, isn't he, Celeste?' Byron pounced. 'He's turned Gemma against Nathan somehow, twisted things, made things look bad for him.'

'That's not true!' Celeste defended.

'Bulldust! I saw the way he looked at her the night of the ball and I know his reputation for seducing other men's wives. Can you swear to me that Gemma's not with Damian at this very moment?'

'I'm not going to swear to anything! I was just trying to do the right thing by ringing and telling you this. I thought if Nathan understood that his wife had uncovered his adultery then he wouldn't go running around Sydney like a chook with his head cut off.'

'You mean you thought he wouldn't force his way into that fortified castle you call a house and strangle Damian with his bare hands. You're a fool, Celeste. A damned fool. I'll relay your message, but God help your brother. Nathan loves Gemma, *really* loves her. He would not be unfaithful to her. There is a reasonable explanation for what she saw, or thought she saw, and I aim to make sure she hears that explanation before your brother does something he's likely to get killed for!'

He slammed the phone down in her ear, so forcefully that she cried out. Celeste dropped the receiver back into place then slumped back on to her pillows.

Oh, God . . .

She should never have become involved, should never have stuck her big nose in where it wasn't wanted. She should definitely never have asked Damian to bring Gemma home tomorrow. Next thing, she would have a furious and possibly violent Nathan on her doorstep.

Celeste contemplated ringing Byron back again and begging him not to say a word but she knew that was useless. Byron wouldn't take any notice. He would possibly take delight in stirring up trouble for her.

Crossing her arms across her eyes, Celeste lay there, aware of her head still spinning and her heart racing. Was it just the wine, or had even talking to Byron done this to her?

God, but I hate that man, she told herself, sitting up abruptly and swinging her feet on to the thick pile carpet. Resisting the silly urge to actually go swimming, Celeste decided she might join Cora in watching that movie. Distraction was desperately needed.

But when she swayed violently on standing up, then almost banged into the bedroom door on the way out of the room, Celeste decided a strong cup of coffee might be better, by which time the movie would have started.

Movies weren't much good when you'd missed the beginning. Perhaps she'd read a book.

Ten minutes later, she was browsing through their extensive library, a mug of steaming black coffee cupped in her hands. Nothing appealed, however. Really, a visit to a bookstore was in order. Classic novels were all very well but there were times when one just wanted to be entertained in a racy, pacy way.

Maybe some music, she decided, leaving the library and wandering along to the lounge-room where the CD and cassette players were located. Selecting a Michael Bolton tape, she slotted it in, pressed play then settled back to simply enjoy.

She was still simply enjoying when the doorbell buzzed, the doorbell connected to the front gates, *not* to the front door. Celeste shot upright from where she'd been lying on the lounge. Good God! Nathan Whitmore. Byron had told him Gemma was here and he'd come to storm the Bastille!

The bell buzzed again, then continuously, as it did when someone leant on it.

Clearly, he was not going to go away. Neither was Cora going to come to the rescue and answer it, because Cora was ensconced away in her room at the back of the house, watching a movie. She wouldn't even *hear* the buzzer.

Squaring her shoulders, Celeste stood up and walked out into the entrance hall where she flicked the button on the security intercom. 'Celeste Campbell speaking,' she said in her best authoritative voice. 'Who is this?'

'It's Byron Whitmore, and you'd better let me in right away or I'm going to huff and puff and blow your bloody house down.'

'Heavens to Betsy,' came her droll reply. 'I'm simply terrified.' Which she actually was, but be damned if she was going to show it!

'Celeste, I'm warning you, I . . .'

'Oh, do shut up, Byron. It's much too late at night for such twaddle. If you'd stayed on the line long enough before, you rude man, I would have been able to tell you that Damian and Gemma are not here. Neither do I know where they are.'

'Prove it! Let me in so that I can see for myself that they're not there.'

'Be my guest!' Celeste snapped, pressing the button that would open the gates. It was only when Byron drove in and actually presented himself at the front door that she remembered how she was dressed. And by then it was too late. If she didn't open the door immediately he would probably batter it down. Or break one of the glass sections.

Wrapping the négligé around her as modestly as she could, she went to the door and opened it. Byron strode straight in, looking devilishly attractive in a casual pair of grey trousers and a sky-blue crew-necked sweater. Looking at him, Celeste could not believe he was fifty. He looked many years younger. He also looked very, very angry.

His glittering blue gaze swept over her, turning mocking and sardonic by the time it reached her fluffy footwear. 'Did I interrupt something? Or do you always go round the house dressed in stuff like that?'

'You interrupted something,' she couldn't resist saying, revelling in his reaction. His whole body stiffened, his nostrils flaring as his nose shot up.

'I was in the middle of being entertained by Michael Bolton,' she added in a low, husky voice. 'Surely you know Michael?'

When Byron remained frozen and silent, she gave a melodramatic sigh. 'I see you don't. Truly, Byron, there is more to music than opera and symphonies, you know. Michael Bolton is a singer. He specialises in love songs.'

Was that relief momentarily flashing across his eyes or had she merely imagined it? What would he have done, she wondered, if a half-naked man had wandered out to see where she was, a handsome, half-naked, very young man? God, she almost regretted firing Gerry, regretted turning down what he'd pressed for that night. It might have been worth it actually to take a real toy-boy lover if she'd known it would have provided such a superb revenge.

'One day, Celeste,' Byron ground out, 'you're going to goad me one time too many.'

'Oh? And what will you do, Byron? Sully your hands on the very thing you most despise? I doubt it. You're too *good* for that,' she spat at him. 'You came to see if Gemma and Damian were here? Come, then. This way for the grand tour. Shall we go upstairs first and check the bedrooms? Yes, I think so...'

She swooshed up the stairs, letting her robe flow free in an act of defiance which he knew was deadly dangerous. But his ongoing contempt for her had sparked an intensely compelling urge that refused to listen to common sense. She ached to push him to the limit, to make him break, one way or the other. And vows she had made about not letting him touch her again seemed irrelevant in the face of her desire to make him eat *his* words, to make him admit that he still wanted her, to make him reach out and try to take what he had once craved as badly as she had.

It was madness. Celeste accepted that. But then, she'd been mad about Byron from the first moment she'd met him. It had merely taken seeing him face to face a couple of times recently to bring it out in her again.

'I'll open the doors for you if you like,' she offered blithely, throwing each one open as she moved briskly along the upstairs hall. She didn't turn her head to find out if Byron actually looked into the rooms or not, but she could hear his footsteps behind her. 'Don't forget to look under the beds,' she called back over her shoulder. 'And in the bathrooms. They might be hiding in one of the showers together. That room's mine. Perhaps you shouldn't go in there if you don't want to contaminate yourself.'

Celeste cried out when Byron's hands suddenly closed over her shoulders, dragging her to a halt and back against him. 'Stop it,' he hissed, his mouth brushing the top of her hair. 'Just stop it.'

'Stop what?' she answered, but her voice was trembling and so was she. Oh, God . . . this wasn't at all what she'd been trying to do. *He* was supposed to end up the victim here, not her own silly self.

But dear heaven, she couldn't stop herself from melting back into him, couldn't stop her head from tipping back against his chest, or her eyes from closing on a ragged sigh of sheer desire.

Byron's tortured groan went some way to soothing her own dismay. Clearly, he couldn't resist the physical contact any more than she could.

'Damn you, Celeste,' he rasped. 'I should have known better than to come here.'

'Touch me, Byron,' she pleaded in a voice she scarcely recognised as her own. 'Touch me . . .'

Another groan escaped his lips as his hands slid from her shoulders down her arms, down past her outstretched fingers and on to her satin-covered thighs. Her heartbeat went wild when his hands moved across her thighs and up over her stomach, massaging its muscular flatness through the slithery material then following the gentle curve of her ribcage till they reached the undersides of her breasts.

When he hesitated at this point, she moaned her disappointment, her own hands lifting to urge his up over the exquisitely swollen curves. When his fingers brushed against the already erect nipples, she gasped, her hips automatically moving against his as everything inside her contracted.

'God, Celeste,' he muttered, his head dipping to suckle ravenously at the tender skin of her throat. His hands were rough on her breasts now, his lips harsh against her flesh. She began to yearn for him, yearn and burn. Her arm lifted to curve up over his shoulders, her hands finding his head, her fingers splaying passionately into the thick black waves. Her own head began to twist round, her mouth blindly searching for his.

'Kiss me,' she rasped.

He spun her round so quickly that her head whirled madly, though it whirled further when his mouth clamped hungrily over hers, when his tongue drove between her softly parted lips so deep that she almost choked. But then his tongue suddenly retreated, and her own followed, diving as boldly into his mouth as his had in hers. The erotic exchange went on for long tempestuous moments till at last he broke away, breathing hard as he glared down into her wildly flushed face.

'I must be crazy,' he grated out. 'But suddenly, I don't care. I want you, god-dammit, and I'm going to have you. I take it there's no objection?' he taunted, bending to scoop her up into his arms.

She stared up at him with wide eyes and he laughed.

'Don't say later you didn't have the chance to say no,' he growled.

She didn't say no. She didn't say anything as he carried her into her bedroom, even when he dumped her unceremoniously into the middle of the bed. If it had been any other man, she would have fought him, would have kicked out at him with deadly accuracy, felling him with one blow.

But this was Byron, the man she loved, the man she had always loved.

Oh, yes, she hated him too, but there was no room in her for hate tonight, not while her body was aflame with a fire it hadn't known in so long. Only Byron could quench that fire, she knew. And so she reached for him, twining her arms around his neck and drawing him down towards her with a tortured moan of sensuous surrender.

'Oh, my darling,' she whispered, with far too much emotion.

She felt his instinctive retreat, felt him fight the same futile fight that they'd both been fighting all day, and then he collapsed upon her, devouring her in an orgy of kissing and touching that might have frightened any other woman.

But Byron's passion had never frightened Celeste. It drove her wild, her hands running over him in the same frantic fashion as his were on her. Her flesh, however, was more accessible than his with what she was wearing,

and soon the satin was bunched up over her hips and he
was stroking bare thighs and buttocks, tangling his fingers in the damp curls between her legs, caressing the
valley they guarded so ineffectually.

'Like silk,' he murmured while she bit her bottom lip
in an effort to stop her moans. 'Or is it honey?'

Celeste gasped a feeble protest when he slid down her
body and started to feed on that honey. But any resistance was token. She could still recall what it had felt like
the first time Byron had done this to her, how her embarrassed shock had quickly changed to an avid willing-
ness to have him do it as often as he liked. Once she'd
even let him do it to her while she was sitting on his desk.
There was nothing like it.

There was still nothing like it, her senses spinning out
as his lips, and tongue moved over her. Desire flared
wildly, then exploded.

'Oh, God,' she cried out, her back arching from the
bed under a series of sharp, electric spasms.

The intensity of her pleasure, however, was mingled
with dismay. She had not wanted it like this. She had
wanted Byron inside her, had wanted to hold him close
and pretend that he loved her. Instead, he seemed almost removed from her, his only touch a brutal grip on
her thighs as he held her open for his rapacious mouth.

Oh, why didn't he stop? she groaned silently. It was
over. Surely he could tell it was over!

But he didn't stop. He went on and on and, amazingly, it wasn't over. The build-up returned, more excru-
ciating than ever, her sensitivity seemingly having moved
up on to a higher plateau. Her blood grew hotter, her
head lighter, her nerve-endings more stretched. There was
another shattering release, and this time, there was no
ebbing of desire. She wanted more. And more. Suddenly, Celeste began to worry he might go on like this
forever. And for all its heady delights, it would not be
enough, not till he came to her properly. Only that would
truly satisfy her. Only that . . .

Tortured words came from her mouth as she struggled to express what she yearned, even as her body betrayed her a third time.

'No more...please...no more...'

His laughter was demonic as he lifted himself from her
and stood to stare down at her body, spread-eagled in
utter abandonment for his desire-filled gaze. 'I haven't
got what *I* want yet, Celeste,' he growled, stripping his
sweater over his head to reveal a bare chest underneath,
a very male chest with broad shoulders and rippling
muscles and a smattering of dark curls across the centre.
'I was just getting you in the right frame of mind.'

His shoes and trousers joined the sweater, followed by
his briefs and socks till he stood before her, still the man
she remembered. Nothing had changed. Nothing had
wilted with the years.

She gave a small shuddering sigh, her eyes closing as
she sat up and reefed her own clothing over her head,
flinging it away before lowering herself back down on to
the satin quilt, her smokily aroused eyes fluttering open
with another sigh that was the very essence of female
sensuality.

Byron's eyes narrowed upon her, his fists closing and
unclosing by his side. 'God, but you're a beautiful bitch,'
he muttered. 'A beautiful brazen bad bitch. But that's all
right. Tonight I want you to be bad, Celeste. Nothing else
will do.'

Celeste gasped when Le moved abruptly on to the bed
to straddle her body. For a few seconds, he knelt tall
above her, dark and dangerous, but then he settled his
weight across her stomach and hips, his knees sinking
into the mattress as he leant forward to present himself
perilously close to her face. When he actually pressed
himself against her mouth, shock sent her jerking backwards and her lips falling slightly apart. But along with
the shock came a wickedly compelling excitement. She
had done this for him once before, but it had been only
very briefly and only as part of foreplay leading to making love. This could hardly be put in the same category.
And yet...

She licked suddenly dry lips, and Byron's gaze was riveted to the movements of her tongue as it moistened her mouth in what must have looked like a blatantly erotic tease. It was, however, the action of suddenly ambivalent emotions. She wanted to, yet she didn't want to. Maybe if she closed her eyes and pretended he still loved her...

'Just do it,' he urged, his hard words giving her nothing of pretence to cling to. This was dominant male demanding from submissive female, maybe even with an underlying intent to humiliate. It went against everything Celeste had vowed never to let happen to her again.

'No,' she choked out, and turned her face away to the side.

She didn't dare look up at him, a tremor of fear rippling through her at the position she realised she was in. Byron was a powerful man. With her body pinned to the bed like this, she had little hope of successfully using her martial art skills against him, not without endangering his life. And did she really want to do that?

She felt his weight tip backwards on to her pelvis, her eyes flinging open to find him sitting down on her and appearing to study the contours of her body, first with his eyes and then with his hands. His strokes were long and sweeping at first. Down and up her sides. Down and up her arms. Then his hands turned over and he started trailing the backs of his fingertips over her by now almost quivering flesh. When his nails trailed over a particularly sensitive spot, she couldn't help an involuntary shudder which brought a grunt of satisfaction from Byron.

Celeste found herself holding her breath when he started moving closer and closer to her breast, sucking in a sharp breath when he skimmed over her nipples. As though sensing she wanted more of this, he stopped doing it, moving his attention to her stomach which proved to have its own brand of erotic torture. Who would have dreamt that a lazy finger encircling one's navel could make all one's muscles clench inside, would make one yearn to take that finger and suck it deep into one's mouth?

But it was when he returned to her breasts in earnest that Celeste knew she was in danger of losing all control. Though only small, especially when she was lying down, her breasts seemed to have swollen to twice their normal size, her nipples almost doubling in length, stretching upwards in a type of pained supplication.

Byron was teasingly slow to oblige, her anticipation so great by the time his head bent to lick one that a violent tremor raced through her. His head lifted and a wickedly rueful smile tugged at his mouth. 'It's agony, isn't it, wanting something so much? Do you want me to do it again, Celeste? All you have to do is say so...'

Their eyes locked and she would have died rather than say it. Byron laughed and bent to torture her some more, first one breast, then the other. Her excitement soared, bringing with it a desire to *do*, rather than just receive. Her hands ran restlessly over his shoulders, her head lifting to kiss the top of his head. She would have moved her lower body if she could have, but only her legs were free to move. They shifted agitatedly on the bed, her knees lifting then falling wantonly apart. Again and again she found herself licking dry lips. If only he would kiss her. If only he would fill her mouth with his. Her lips fell softly apart on a raw moan.

And then he was there, and she was taking him in, and there was no thought of saying no again, no thought of stopping, no thought of anything except doing what he wanted, what *she* wanted.

Dimly she heard Byron's groan of dark triumph. And then she heard nothing, her senses whirling into the eye of an erotic storm which could only end one way.

CHAPTER SEVEN

CELESTE leant against the marble vanity-unit, then slowly lifted her face to the mirror. How could I have allowed that? she asked herself shakily. More to the point, how could I have *enjoyed* it?

She shook her head, dropping her eyes back into the basin and the water still swirling there. Snapping off the still running tap, Celeste turned away before she caught another glimpse of that humiliating reflection with its flushed cheeks and overbright eyes.

Pride battled with her ongoing desire. You can't go back out there, she lectured herself. You just can't! What must he think of you to demand such an intimacy without love? What must he think of you now that you have given it to him, seemingly without love?

Oh, God ...

Celeste's head dropped into her hands, self-disgust beginning to override everything—till that old familiar tape clicked into play and she remembered everything that he had done to her, everything he had set in motion. Byron might still be her Achilles' heel in a sexual sense, but he didn't have to be in any other way. OK, so she loved him somewhere down deep in her psyche, but she hated him at the same time. He might think he could use her again, but she would prove him wrong there. If anyone was to be doing the using this time, it would be her.

Picking up a hairbrush, she took her hair down out of the combs that kept it back from her face and brushed it out till it tumbled in wild waves around her shoulders and halfway down her back. There seemed little point in putting lipstick on her pink puffy lips so she merely sprayed some perfume over her totally naked body, took a deep breath and opened the bathroom door.

A pair of wintry blue eyes surveyed her nakedness as she walked across the plush-pile carpet. Not that he could make any comment when he was lying in the nude on top of her bed, his arms linked nonchalantly behind his head.

'Are you planning on staying the night?' she asked as she bent over with seeming nonchalance and picked up the robe of the négligé set. She slid her arms into the silky sleeves and did her best to resist the urge to pull it tightly around her. 'For if you are, I'll go down and lock up.'

When he didn't say anything, she was forced to look over at him. Suddenly, the expression on his face infuriated her. How dared he lie there in judgement of her? How dared he look at her with that hard gleam of contempt in his eyes?

As always, her only satisfaction lay in apparent indifference to what he thought or felt about her. After all, she already knew he still wanted her as much as ever. She also doubted he would be able to resist the temptation to stay and taste whatever other delights he thought she offered all her lovers. That in itself was sweet vengeance.

A softly mocking smile teased her mouth as she drifted back towards the bed, the action of walking sending the robe floating back from its centre parting. She exulted in the way his eyes became riveted to her body, and the triangle of dark curls at the junction of her groin. She sat down on the bed, and crossed her legs, leaning over to place a provocative hand on his nearest thigh, then running it up over his body till it rested on his chest. His heart was hammering like mad beneath her hand and she knew he was hers, whenever she wanted him. He'd crossed a line tonight and she would never let him go back.

'I want you to stay,' she whispered huskily. 'Please, darling...'

His eyes flashed with the endearment, his hands whipping down to snatch her wrists and pull her up on to his body.

'You bitch,' he rasped. 'You'll pay for this. I don't
know how, but you will.'

'Maybe I already have ...'

He laughed. 'And what was the price?'

'I've never been able to assess it. What price do you
put on one's sanity, or one's life?'

He frowned at this, his hands tightening around her
wrists as he dragged her further up on to him. 'What the
hell are you talking about?'

'That's what I'm talking about. Hell. A living hell.'

He laughed again. 'Yes, that's what you are all right,
Celeste. A living, breathing hell. You've never been any
different. Even when you were little more than a child,
you were the devil's child, tempting me, corrupting me.'

'Corrupting *you*?' she scoffed. 'I was only seventeen,
for pity's sake. You were twenty-seven. Who was the
corrupter, I ask you?'

His face darkened with fury. 'Don't try to blame me,
Celeste. You know damned well what you did. You found
every excuse to come into my office those two weeks. You
wore the most exotic perfume I've ever smelt on a female. You never wore a bra. Sometimes I wondered if
you had *any* underwear on. You flicked those cat's eyes
of yours my way all the time and you let me know with
every movement of your lush, nubile young body that I
could have you whenever I wanted you.'

An irritatingly guilty heat flamed in her cheeks. Yes,
she had been provocative. She had to admit that. But
she'd been in love, dammit. She'd adored the man. How
else was she to get him to notice her when he could have
any woman he wanted? She had to show them that *she*
was a woman, or nearly one.

'I see you agree with me,' Byron snarled, seeing her
betraying blush.

'I do not!' she snapped. 'I was a silly young girl, I admit, but only silly because I was in love. You took advantage of me, Byron. You made me think you loved me.'

'*I* made *you* think I loved you!' he exploded, rolling
her over and spreading her arms wide on the pillows, his
grip quite brutal on her flesh. Once again, she was pinned

to the mattress, and once again, her skills of self-defence were useless. 'That's a laugh. I would have said the very opposite was true if it didn't make me look a fool. Not that you didn't make a fool of me back then, Celeste. It was only after you'd gone back to school and I found out what an experienced little seducer of older men you already were that I appreciated the extent of my stupidity. You say you were in love with me. Well, you seem to fall in love a lot, don't you, Celeste? Is it that you need to tell yourself you're in love to justify what you do with me?'

Celeste's eyes widened at his astonishing accusations, her heart racing. 'What do you mean, I was already an experienced seducer of men? You were my first lover.'

'Oh, for pity's sake, Celeste, even if Irene hadn't told me all about you, I still knew there'd been others before me. You were no virgin when I made love to you that day in the office.'

Celeste bit her lip as she realised that that awful incident when she'd been only fourteen would have destroyed her technical virginity. Even the doctor who examined her back then had waffled over the possible extent of her sexual activity. When she'd reported the teacher for attempted rape, he had claimed she'd been more than co-operative, then another teacher on the staff had backed him up by saying the same thing about her.

It had been a conspiracy, of course, for the first man to escape retribution for his vile act. The two men had been devils in arms and she had unfortunately left it a couple of weeks before reporting the frightening incident. By then any damage to her young body had healed and she was left with no evidence of forcible entry.

Her mother had believed her, however, taking her away from that school and putting her in another. She'd also put her on the Pill for safety, aware that Celeste had the sort of looks men found it hard to resist.

'What...what did Irene tell you?' she asked shakily, staring up into Byron's glittering blue eyes.

'The truth! That you'd slept with half the male staff at your school when you were only fourteen. That you were expelled and that your mother had to put you on the Pill because she was scared you'd be pregnant before you were fifteen, you were so sex-mad. From the way you acted with me, she did the wise thing.'

'And what if I said I didn't sleep with those teachers or any other men before you? What if I told you one of the teachers tried to rape me, that he actually had me on the ground before I kneed him in the groin and got away?'

'What would you say if I said your behaviour over the years hardly backs up that story?' he countered savagely. 'You're verging on being a nymphomaniac, Celeste. Admit it. You are sex-mad. Over the years you've craved younger and younger men because they can probably last longer and can do it more often. But let me assure you, sweetheart, I'm not done yet tonight. I'll give you what you crave.'

He used his massive legs to push hers apart, settling his weight between her thighs. Without letting her arms go he began to probe with his body. Celeste tried not to feel anything as his desire rubbed and pressed against hers, but she could not prevent the exciting sensations he was evoking or the way her blood began to pound in her head.

She sucked in a sharp breath when he finally achieved success, gasping when he drove his desire home to the hilt.

'This is what you want, isn't it, Celeste?' he said through gritted teeth, surging into her again and again. 'But it's not love. It's pure unadulterated lust. Say it like it is for once, Celeste. Tell the truth and shame the devil. You want this, and only this...'

Her body convulsing uncontrollably around his made him cry out with raw satisfaction. His back arched away, his hands pressing her wrists down in the pillows as his own arms straightened. And then he was pulling her up from the bed, keeping their spasming bodies fused together as he sat back on his heels. With a tortured groan, he released her wrists to wrap his arms around her, clasping her close and rocking her to and fro, his head dropping to bury his face in her hair. Reaching up her back, he grasped a clump of hair, pulling her head back so that he could feed on her throat like some ravenous animal.

Celeste was beside herself with the awful ambivalence of the sharpest emotional pain yet the fiercest of sexual satisfactions. To have the man you loved find such pleasure in your body, despite his despising you, had a kind of perverted triumph to it. Celeste chose to lock on to this bittersweet victory, rather than any crippling despair, for she'd long learnt that there was no future in harbouring hurt over Byron's opinion of her, just as there was no point in arguing with him over Irene's lies.

Byron would never believe her version of events, just as he would never believe the truth about the way she'd lived her life since. She'd been hoist by her own petard and she would just have to live with it.

At least there was some consolation in a new understanding of the events on that day in the billiard-room at Belleview, two years after he married Irene. Byron hadn't been quite the callous bastard she'd always believed him to be, merely a man torn apart by unwanted feelings for a girl he thought unworthy of anything but the basest treatment.

Which was how he'd treated her that day, taking what she had unconsciously offered him again, then scorning her afterwards when she broke down and told him how much she loved him. It was at that point that Irene had walked in, taken one look at their guilty faces then left the room, whereupon Byron had launched forth into a bitter tirade.

'I'll never forgive myself for hurting a good woman over a slut like you,' he'd flung at her. 'And you dare to speak of love. That wasn't love you gave me on the billiard-table just now, you little tramp. It was the same thing you give every man who looks sideways at you. I'm married, for pity's sake, to your own sister. Doesn't that mean anything to you? Haven't you any decency at all? God, you disgust me, almost as much as I disgust myself for being too weak to resist your insidious appeal. Go and screw up some other poor bastard's life, not mine! I don't want to set eyes on you again, do you hear me? Get out,

out of this house and out of my life. I can't stand the sight of you any longer!'

Much as she had never forgotten those words, nor forgiven them, Celeste could now understand them a little better.

Besides, she thought with a black satisfaction, whose arms is he in now? Whose bed is he in? Whose body can't he keep his hands and eyes off?

Mine!

Celeste ran tantalising fingertips over his sweat-slicked back, squeezing her muscles tightly around him, teasing him back to arousal once again. With the quickening of his flesh, she began to lift her hips in tiny up and down movements, gripping and releasing him till he was fully erect again.

'Yes,' she insisted huskily when he groaned. She pushed him back on to the bed, holding his shoulders down while she straddled him as mercilessly as he had straddled her. This time she was on top and she aimed to keep it that way, riding him as relentlessly and ruthlessly as he had her, closing her eyes so that she didn't see his contempt.

'Yes,' she cried out in exultation when his body finally arched up and exploded into her. 'Yes,' she sobbed as her own body shattered into pieces and she collapsed in a spent heap across his chest.

Did they sleep? They must have, limbs tangled, bodies exhausted.

Celeste snapped awake to the sound of Cora calling out to her up the stairs.

'Are you still awake, Celeste? Shall I lock up for you?'

Celeste lifted her head and spoke in a stunningly calm voice, even though her heart was instantly pounding. Dear God, what if Cora had come up and found her like this? They'd left the bedroom door open, the bed in full view of anyone who even walked past.

'It's all right, Cora. I'll do it. I'll be down shortly to have a nightcap. You go to bed.'

'OK. The movie was pretty awful, by the way. Good-night, then.'

'Goodnight.'

Celeste closed her eyes with a relieved sigh, opening them to find Byron looking up at her with that familiar mocking cynicism in his eyes. 'I see you have your housekeeper trained never to come upstairs, or to ask sticky questions. I dare say she's used to you having every Tom, Dick and Harry spend the night.'

'Don't you mean Luke, Gerry and Byron?' she retorted. Celeste had already made up her mind not to try to defend herself to Byron. It was a waste of time. Neither was she going to let him treat her like dirt, or ride roughshod over her emotions. 'Naturally, I don't have to answer to my housekeeper, Byron. Do you ever answer to yours?'

'I don't have a housekeeper any more, as you very well know.'

'Ah, yes. The gorgeous Melanie flew off with that racing-car driver, didn't she?' Is that why you started running around with Catherine Whatsername? Because your live-in lady found alternative outlets for her—er—needs?'

With a low growl, Byron heaved Celeste from his body and threw himself on to his feet, glaring down at her with fury in his face. 'Just because you have all your employees service you, Celeste, it doesn't mean everyone else does.' He snatched up his trousers and started dragging them on.

'Don't you think you should put your underpants on first?' Celeste suggested sweetly.

Byron told her not so sweetly what he thought of her suggestion, zipping up his trousers so angrily that she winced. He rammed the blue sweater roughly over his head, combing his hair back into place with splayed fingers before sitting down on the edge of the bed to put on his shoes and socks.

Celeste knelt up behind him, draping her arms around his shoulders and kissing him on the ear. 'Don't be angry, darling. I don't care what you did with Melanie.'

'I didn't do anything!'

'You must have thought about it. She was very beautiful.'

Celeste felt she had struck a nerve for he definitely stiffened. 'I have no intention of defending my thoughts. I never touched the woman.'

'Good for you. I'm glad to see you're still as virtuous as ever. When am I going to see you again?'

'Never, if I can help it.'

Her laughter was drily amused. 'Don't be silly, darling. You enjoyed yourself tonight as much as I did. Why, I haven't been this impressed since...since we were last together.'

'God, don't remind me of that. I've been trying to forget that day for the last twenty-one years.'

'You and me both,' she muttered under her breath, and shrank back on her heels.

Byron turned to stare at her. 'If I didn't know better, I'd think you regretted that day as much as I did.'

'Oh, yes, Byron, I still regret it. Bitterly.'

He seemed surprised. 'You might be more human than I thought you were.'

Her smile was ironic, her pleasure warped as she wriggled on to his lap, snaking her arms around his chest and kissing him with tantalising softness on the mouth. 'I'm very human,' she whispered, and ran her tonguetip over his lips.

His groan thrilled her.

'When am I going to see you again?' she tempted a second time. 'If you don't come to me, I'll come to you. You do know that, don't you?'

'Yes,' he bit out.

'Take me out to dinner tomorrow night.'

'You have to be joking! I won't be seen in public with you. I'm not going to make a laughing-stock of myself for the sake of this.'

'For the sake of what?'

'This!' he snarled, and crushed her to him, taking her mouth in a savage kiss that branded his feelings for what they were: lust. Nothing more. They had never been

anything more. He knew it and she knew it. But the realisation still had the power to bring pain.

Celeste pushed him away and scrambled off his lap to
stand with her hands on her hips. 'Then to hell with you,
Byron Whitmore! I'm not some cheap whore to be visited in the dead of night down some dark alley. Whatever you pretend in public, you're no better than me, are
you? You're here and you wanted me as much as, if not
more than, I wanted you.'

Byron's mouth twisted, his face hardening at her accusation. 'Yes,' he admitted with a healthy does of bitter remorse. 'But I'm not proud of it.'

'Why not?'

He threw her a disbelieving glance.

'You're a normal man, aren't you?' she taunted. 'Well,
a normal man has normal male desires. Surely you're not
going to tell me you've only been holding hands with
Catherine Whatsername? No, I didn't think so. Your
wife's dead, Byron, which means you're either going to
be celibate for the rest of your life, marry again, have
one-night stands or come to a sensible arrangement with
some co-operative woman. Who better than me? As for
the gossip-mongers... They'll have a field-day for a
whole week, but if you don't react they'll forget you and
me and move on elsewhere.'

'And what of my family?' he pointed out scornfully.
'You're not exactly well liked around Belleview.
Nathan, for one, detests you. He... Oh, my God,
Nathan! I forgot all about him and Gemma. Hell, I for-
got everything!' He jumped to his feet and glared at her.
'I usually do whenever I go anywhere near you, don't I?
What is it? Have you cast a spell on me? Sold your soul
to the devil in exchange for mine? Damn you, cover
yourself up! How can I have a sensible discussion with
you when you stand there, flaunting yourself at me?'

Celeste shrugged, but wrapped the robe more modestly around herself. 'You can't live your life by what
others think, Byron.'

His laughter was rueful. 'You certainly don't.'

'No, I don't. People will believe whatever they want to anyway.'

'Are you referring to me?'

'Among others. You're no better than all those narrow-minded little people who gobble up everything they read in the tabloids without stopping to question a thing. They love reading dirt and believing dirt. It's so very easy to make the general public think very badly of you. So very, very easy.'

Byron was frowning at her. 'You make it sound like you deliberately set out to make that happen.'

'Maybe I have . . .'

'Why would you do that?' he jeered.

'Why not? Maybe it amused me. Good God, Byron, if I'd had as many lovers as the papers and magazines suggested I had, I wouldn't have had time to do any work. I'd have been flat on my back all the time.'

'Or on your knees,' he sneered.

Her hand flashed out to crack him a beauty around the face. 'Don't you ever say that to me again. I have never done that for any other man, do you hear me? Not a one!'

Immediately scepticism flittered across his eyes, quickly followed by a definite doubt, then finally a troubled acceptance of the truth. 'I see no reason for you to lie to me about that, so I apologise.'

'Apology accepted,' she choked out, blinking madly as her eyes filled with unexpected tears.

This only made his frown deepen. 'I've really upset you, haven't I?' he said with surprise in his voice.

'It doesn't matter.'

'Of course it does. I . . . I guess I forgot . . .'

'Forgot what?'

'That you are still a human being,' he said gently. 'With feelings.'

That almost did it.

Celeste's only salvation was to walk away so that he couldn't see the blurring in her eyes and the torment in her face. Gathering herself quickly as she walked, she was able to turn when she reached the open doorway, a cool mask in place. 'I think you'd better go.'

He sighed. 'Yes. I think I'd better.'

'You can tell Nathan with a clear conscience that Gemma is not here.'

'And you honestly don't know where she is?'

'No, I do not. To be honest I regret becoming involved at all. Gemma and Nathan are nothing to me.'

'Damian is your brother. If he's involved, then so will you be.'

'I don't see it that way. Damian's an adult. I'm not responsible for what he does. I think you would be wise to adopt a similar attitude with Nathan. His marriage is his marriage. He won't appreciate your interference.'

'You could be right. But since Gemma hasn't seen fit to tell him what she thinks she saw, I have no option but to do so.'

'Maybe. But after that, it's up to Nathan to fight his own battles. But let me give you a bit of female advice. If he's been unfaithful to her, then I don't like his chances.'

'Not all wives throw out their husbands for one lapse,' he said pointedly.

Celeste smiled. It was not a nice smile. 'If you're referring to darling Irene, then not all women are as forgiving and Christian as my sweet half-sister, are they?'

'Are you being sarcastic, Celeste?'

'Of course I'm being bloody sarcastic, Byron!' she stormed. 'God, you were as blind about her as you were about everything else. Didn't you ever find out what a bitch she was? What an evil, manipulative, cruel bitch?'

Byron stared at her.

'Just ask Ava! Or Jade! Or anyone else other than your own stupid self. You married a monster, Byron. Oh, yes, she loved you, much more than she hated everyone else!'

Celeste laughed as he continued to stare at her. 'I suppose I shouldn't be too hard on you. You're just a man, after all. What man can resist having a woman who is willing to play any role to fit the occasion and flatter his ego? Blushing virgin fiancé, then adoring bride, and finally the understanding and ever-sacrificing wife. I wouldn't have believed any of it if I hadn't seen it for myself. But she couldn't keep it up, could she? In the end her dark side came to the fore, didn't it?'

'I don't want to hear this,' he muttered.

'I'm sure you don't. Who wants to hear the awful truth?'

'She was a sick woman. I know that. But I couldn't throw her away, could I? Not after I—'

'Done her wrong?' Celeste broke in scoffingly.

Byron's eyes narrowed. 'Yes,' he bit out. 'I should never have married her.'

'You didn't love her, did you?'

'No.'

Celeste's heart contracted, just before it swelled with a heart-wrenching emotion. 'I knew you didn't love her,' she said in a strangled voice. 'How could you? You loved *me!*'

'Loved *you!*' he spluttered. 'I never loved *you*. You were nothing but a...a sickness! One I don't seem to have developed an immunity for. But at least now my sickness doesn't have to hurt anyone else. I have that salve for my conscience. And who knows? Maybe if I have you often enough this time, this damnable fire that has tormented me all these years might burn itself out at long last!'

For a few agonising seconds this new but equally brutal rejection of her love almost did what his earlier rejections had not succeeded in doing. But at the last moment, Celeste gathered herself, a bitter little smile curving her mouth.

'Oh, I doubt that, Byron,' she drawled. 'I doubt that very much. However, I suggest you do go home now. I've had enough of you for tonight. But we'll never be finished. Not while there's breath in my body. Let yourself out. I'll lock up later.'

Her smile faded once she'd made it into the bathroom and shut the door. There, she surveyed herself in the mirror with narrowed eyes and clenched jaw. It had been imperative, of course, that she not break down again. If she had, nothing would have saved her. Not drugs, or doctors, or anything.

Of course she should never have slept with Byron again. It had opened a Pandora's box of emotions that were dangerously difficult to control.

But that didn't mean she wouldn't do her damnedest to control them. She might still love and desire the man, but she also hated and despised him. It was a volatile mixture, one which would need the most careful of handling if she was to survive unscarred for a second time.

And Celeste meant to survive. Oh, yes . . . she hadn't come this far to go under now. If there was to be a victim this time, it wasn't going to be her!

After a few minutes, Celeste exited from the bathroom to find the bedroom blessedly empty. So was the rest of the house. Byron's car was no longer in the driveway.

She closed the front gates, locked up, then went back upstairs to have a relaxing shower and climb into bed, where she did her best to will herself into a calm, restful sleep.

But Celeste was to find that sleep was one thing she was powerless to control. So were her dreams. When sheer exhaustion finally claimed her in the early hours of the morning, her mind was filled with nightmares in which a face came back to haunt her from the past, a hard sculpted face with chilling blue eyes and a granite jaw and fists like iron.

CHAPTER EIGHT

CELESTE was in conference with Luke, briefing him further on his new position, when the red light on her desk winked on. With a tut-tut of irritation, she flicked the switch on her intercom system and leant forward.

'Yes, Ruth?' she asked the temp she'd had sent over this morning from an agency Campbell's always used.

'A Mr Whitmore to see you, Ms Campbell.'

Celeste's stomach clenched down hard. Byron hadn't waited long to inform Nathan, it seemed. And Nathan hadn't taken long in showing up. Dear God, the last thing she wanted today was to have to placate some irrational and potentially violent husband. Not only did she have serious business on her plate, but she felt emotionally fragile. Still, Nathan was unlikely to simply go away, and she didn't think it would be wise if she asked him to wait.

'Show Mr Whitmore in, Ruth.'

'Yes, Ms Campbell.'

'Sorry, Luke,' she apologised as she got to her feet. 'Here. Take these sales analyses and see for yourself where our weaknesses lie, then start formulating a plan to redress matters, both short-term and long-term.'

Luke took the huge pile of computer printouts and threw her one of his little-used smiles, one which quite transformed his face from ordinary to extremely attractive. The smile still lingered on his face as he turned and met Mr Whitmore on his way in.

Not Nathan Whitmore, Celeste saw to her intense dismay. Byron Whitmore.

She froze, the events of last night seeming not only more shocking in the cold light of day, but almost unreal. Looking at Byron standing there in his navy pinstriped suit, the very essence of dignified respectability, made it difficult to cope with the images that kept popping into her mind. Her salvation was the sardonic expression that slid into his bright blue eyes as they raked over the smiling Luke.

'Thank you, Ruth,' she said dismissively to the secretary. 'I'll see you later, Luke,' she added in deliberate defiance of Byron's presence. 'We'll have lunch together. Book somewhere near, would you?'

To give him credit, Luke accepted these sudden arrangements with casual aplomb. Celeste realised she had found a gem in that young man.

The office door closed behind the departing people and Celeste was left to stare across the room at the man she both loved and hated.

'I take it *that* Luke is the Luke you referred to last night?' he said with cool derision.

'Of course.'

'You're sleeping with him?'

'Actually, no. Not yet. Cats like to play with their mice for a while first.'

'I'm no mouse, Celeste,' he warned darkly. 'You play with me at your own risk.'

'Maybe risk turns me on, Byron,'

'What doesn't?' he sneered.

'Losing.'

Darting her a black look, he slid his hands into the pockets of his trousers and began to pace to and fro across the dark green carpet in front of her desk. 'I haven't come here to indulge in smart-arse repartee, Celeste. I've come for some answers.'

Celeste sighed and sat back down in her large black leather swivel chair. 'I told you before, Byron. I do not know where Damian and Gemma are. You've wasted your time coming here. I cannot be browbeaten into confessing something I don't know.'

When Byron ground to a halt in front of her desk, his dark brows bunched together in a troubled frown, Celeste found herself staring at his firm male mouth and remembering the pleasure it had given her the previous evening. She squirmed on the leather chair, hating her vulnerability to this man almost as much as she found it exciting and irresistible.

'I haven't come here about Nathan,' he said curtly.

Celeste forced herself to sit still and think clearly. 'You haven't told him yet about why Gemma left him?'

'Yes, I told him.'

'And?'

'I let him think she'd contacted me and told me why she'd left,' he admitted grudgingly. 'I had to lie and say she hung up without telling me any real details and that I had no idea where she'd temporarily run off to.'

'And that satisfied him?'

'I wouldn't describe Nathan's reaction as satisfied. Frankly, I didn't understand his reaction at all! If I didn't know better I'd say he was relieved, which hardly makes sense.'

'No, it doesn't. What man would be relieved to find out his wife believes he's cheating on her? What other dark secrets does he have on his conscience, I wonder...?'

'God, not you too. Ava's been giving me curry over this as well. She heard me on the phone to Nathan. When I was forced to admit Gemma had left Nathan she ripped right into Nathan's character. Why does everyone speak so badly of him? What's he ever done to deserve such treatment?'

'Aside from his rather colourful background, Byron, he did divorce his wife and marry a girl almost young enough to be his daughter.'

'Lenore divorced him, god-dammit! She and Nathan only ever married in the first place because she was pregnant with Kirsty. As for Gemma...I can well understand his becoming besotted with someone young like her. She was innocent, you see, innocent and untouched. The complete opposite to that rotten mother of his, and that other old tart who got hold of him when he was only a boy. Good God, why can't people appreciate what a fantastic job he's done of turning his life around? The man's a credit to himself!'

'And to you?'

'No, not to me! I didn't do all that much. He did it all himself.'

'You gave him a home, Byron. And you loved him. Love can heal a lot of wounds.'

Byron didn't seem to hear the sad irony in her words, sweeping on with his usual insensitivity. 'Which is why I want you to get a message to Gemma if you can. That girl loves Nathan. I know she does. She would forgive him anything.'

'Even adultery?'

'He swore blind he'd not been having an affair with Lenore. Apparently, she *had* been at his flat on the Sunday, which was stupid of him, I suppose. But he says he was helping her rehearse a difficult section of the play which opens this Friday. He thinks Gemma might have jumped to conclusions because he was also with Lenore at my party last Friday night. He can see it must have looked bad but all he wants is a chance to explain.'

'I wonder if he'd give her the chance to explain if the situation was reversed?' Celeste mused aloud.

'Of course he would,' Byron stated pompously. 'Why wouldn't he?'

'Because men don't always want to hear women's explanations. They're princes at jumping to conclusions. A lot of girls who are merely silly are branded sluts without a trial, without even a hearing.'

'Are you referring to yourself, Celeste? To *me*?'

Celeste surveyed his blustering anger with a wry ruefulness. 'Of course not, Byron. Why would I do that? You didn't jump to conclusions about me, did you? You simply believed what the woman who loved you told you. What motive would she possibly have had to lie?'

'Why are you taking this stance after all these years?' he asked, throwing his hands up in the air with a frustrated groan. 'You can't honestly expect me to believe you were a total innocent that first time—or later. If that was so, then why have you led such a decadent life since then? All those young men! A few weeks ago it was your

chauffeur. Now you've set your sights on that poor bastard who just left here. God, I pity him!'

'Why? I'm going to look after Luke very well. He's
going places around here.'

'He sure is! Right into your bed!'

'Not for a while, Byron,' she informed him silkily.

'Why the delay? Why not invite him home tonight,
with us? I'm sure it won't be the first time you've had
more than one man at a time.'

A pained outrage sent colour to her cheeks and fury
pulsing through her veins. But when she spoke, her words
were laced with an icy venom that refused to deny his vile
accusation. 'And if I have, what's it to you? You don't
really care about me. All you've ever wanted from me is
what you got last night, so don't give me any more of
your holier-than-thou crap. I'm the only one who's ever
cared in this relationship. I loved you, Byron Whitmore,
and I've no intention of letting you off the hook by letting you believe otherwise!'

'Don't be so bloody ridiculous!' he rapped out. 'You
never loved me, Celeste. You merely wanted me. But I
became the one who got away, the one who wouldn't
dance indefinitely to your tune. You've shown your true
colours since then by surrounding yourself with a whole
string of sexual puppets. But you've finally grown bored
with them, haven't you? That's the answer I was looking
for today, and the reason for last night. You need a real
man again to satisfy you, a man who can control you,
who can call all your bluffs and put you in your place.'

'And where is that?'

'Under *me*.'

'You're an arrogant, presumptuous pig!'

His laughter sent a chill running down her spine and
excitement along her veins. 'I've got your measure,
Celeste. You can't fool me any more. Don't even try.'

She flushed at the way he started looking her over.
Despite the fact that she was dressed in a severely tai-
lored business suit which hid her body well, his desire-
filled gaze sent goose-bumps racing all over her skin. Her

nipples peaked hard against the silk lining of the jacket and she felt the pull of her own desire between his thighs.

'You were right when you said last night that we haven't finished yet,' he said in a low, threatening voice. 'But you were wrong to assume you had the controlling hand in this. Your fires for me are as hot as mine for you. Maybe even hotter. If they weren't, you'd have thrown me out by now. After all, I'm well aware of your capabilities in throwing out a man. I saw you in action at the ball.'

'Something you'd be wise not to forget,' she countered, but rather shakily, she thought.

His smug smile confirmed it. 'You had plenty of opportunity to use your skills on me last night but you didn't. That's rather telling in itself, don't you think?'

When Byron started moving around the large desk, Celeste stiffened back in her chair, her eyes flinging wide. 'Don't you dare touch me,' she rasped.

He swung her chair round to face him, placing a hand on each armrest, effectively imprisoning her in her seat. 'You can always kick me in the groin,' he suggested drily. 'No? Then I'll take your lack of retaliation for an open invitation.' And he bent to kiss her quivering mouth.

Celeste detested the way her heart leapt at this lightest of kisses, but she was quick to resign herself to the situation. Byron was right. Resistance to his sexual approaches was a waste of time. Humiliating too if she tried to fight them, only to surrender eventually like some wimpish victim.

Her lips pulled back into a sexy smile under his, her eyes glittering boldly as they stared right into his. 'Do you think you might wait till lunchtime?' she murmured seductively. 'I'll cancel my lunch with Luke and meet you somewhere.'

Her swift change of tack threw him somewhat, his head drawing back while his eyes narrowed with suspicion. 'Such as where?'

'Don't you have a company suite at the Regency?'

Byron stood up straight, his arms swinging back to his sides as he took a backward step. 'How do you know that?' he asked sharply.

'I know everything about Whitmore's.'

He gave a sarcastic snort. 'You never did fight fair, did you? Your coming into the billiard-room that day in that minuscule bikini was downright wicked. When you actually kissed me, I had no chance, did I?'

Celeste let out a ragged sigh. 'You might not believe this, Byron, but seduction was the last thing on my mind that day. I was trying to make up my mind about something. I kissed you because I wanted to find out if I was over you.'

He laughed. 'You got more then you bargained for, then, didn't you?'

'I certainly did,' she said bitterly. 'For someone who proclaimed that he didn't want to rake over old coals, you have a habit of doing so.'

'I guess I like to keep reminding myself of the type of woman I'm dealing with.'

'Oh? And what type is that?'

'Ruthless. Conscienceless. Vindictive.'

'Vindictive.'

'Do you think I don't know why you revived that old feud between the Campbells and the Whitmores? It had nothing to do with what happened between our fathers. It was because of you and me, Celeste. I rejected you and you couldn't take it. You were the classic woman scorned. You set out to make me pay any way you could. And you succeeded. You succeeded very well. You almost brought Whitmore's to its financial knees. You also worked damned hard to make sure I never forgot what you were like to make love to. You flaunted your sexuality for all the world to see, but you didn't want the world to see it, did you? You only wanted me to see it.'

A wry lop-sided smile curved her scarlet-glossed mouth as she rose from the chair. Byron stood his ground as she pressed herself against him, but Celeste had the immense satisfaction of feeling his shoulders square back, seeing the flash of near panic in his eyes. Oh, how easily she could turn the tables on him. How very easily.

'You could be right, darling,' she purred, snaking her arms up around his neck and standing up on tiptoe to run her tongue-tip over his stiffly held mouth. 'You see, I've never found a man who can do for me what you do. You're the best, Byron. The very best. I don't think I will ever get tired of making love to you . . .'

His groan as he crushed her to him echoed in his ears, his impassioned kiss going some way to blocking the unbearable pain he had unwittingly evoked again. When he finally tore his mouth away he sounded as if he'd run a very long, very hard race. She was merely in a daze. Their power over each other was getting worse, she realised. Where would it all end?

'Be there at one,' he muttered thickly into her hair.

He didn't wait for an answer. He gave her one last impassioned glance then strode from the room, leaving the door open behind him. She walked over and shut it, shuddering as she leant with her back against it. Her eyes went to the clock on the wall. Ten o'clock. One was three long hours away.

SHE LAY NAKED in his arms, her head lying in the crook of his left arm, his free hand lazily tracing patterns over her very relaxed body.

Celeste opened heavy eyes to glance idly around the hotel bedroom. Their clothes lay tidily folded up on adjacent chairs, the sight of them bringing a rueful smile to her lips.

She had insisted on undressing him herself, doing it slowly and methodically, then making him climb into the bed while she undressed herself. There had been no attempt at any erotic striptease. Celeste had been desperately trying to keep control over what was becoming more and more an uncontrollable situation for her. She hadn't been able to work all morning, her thoughts on nothing but being with Byron again.

By the time she had climbed into that bed with him she'd wanted him immediately. Fortunately, his need had been similar and they had come together without any preliminaries. Now they lay together, two spent forces, waiting for the wanting to begin again. Celeste didn't think it would be long.

'You haven't asked me to use anything,' Byron murmured as he stroked her. 'Is that wise?'

Celeste cringed at the implication he was making. It was a perfectly understandable question, considering her reputation, but she still reacted badly to it. 'For you or for me?' came her stiff reply.

'Just answer the question, Celeste. I always used protection with Catherine. Have you been practising safe sex as well?'

'Very safe,' she said drily, thinking that not doing it at all was the safest sex she knew of.

'I'm not talking about just being on the Pill,' he muttered.

'I'm not on the Pill.'

Every muscle in his body froze. 'Isn't that rather dangerous? I'm not too old to become a father, you know. Neither are you too old to become a mother.'

Celeste slipped out of Byron's arms and sat up. 'I can't have any...' She broke off before the word *more* slipped out. 'I can't have any children,' she said tautly, then stood up. 'I'm going to have a shower.'

She was under the hot jets of water when Byron slid back the glass door. 'How long have you known that?' he asked brusquely.

Not looking at him, she closed her eyes and tipped her face up into the water. 'Quite a while.' There was no way he could see her tears with the water beating into her eyes.

He swore, and when she finally opened her eyes he was gone. Five minutes later, she returned to the room, wrapped in a towel. Byron was lying under the sheet on the bed, looking pensive.

'Why didn't you tell me?'

'Why should I?' She dropped the towel and slipped under the sheet next to him. When he gathered her in close, she shivered.

'Because it explains so much,' he rasped. 'A woman who can't have children can do strange things. How did it happen, Celeste? Did you have an abortion and it went wrong? Was that it? Don't be afraid to tell me. I'll try to understand. Really I will.'

Something inside Celeste shattered. Against all common sense and everything she'd vowed, she started to weep.

'God, Celeste,' Byron groaned, and held her close, stroking her back. 'Don't. Please don't. I . . . I can't handle it. It's not like you to cry.'

Rolling her over, he cupped her face and began kissing the tears from her eyes and then her cheeks till, with a muffled moan, he took her mouth with his, drinking in her sobs, biting at her lips and sucking on her tongue with a wildness that stunned her. Clinging to him, she begged silently for his compassion, not passion, but instead he surged deep into her body, surged till she was forced to forget, to think of nothing but his flesh filling hers, till her cries were the cries of a pained release, her moans the moans of despair.

Afterwards, she refused to say any more on the subject of her barren state, no matter how often he asked, dressing quietly and going back to work. If Luke looked at her oddly a couple of times when they met later in the afternoon, at least he had the sense to say nothing.

At five, Celeste had been about to pack up for the day and call a taxi, when Byron telephoned.

'Have dinner with me tonight,' he urged.

Celeste's eyes squeezed tightly shut as her heart skipped a beat. 'Aren't you afraid of being seen with me in public?' she returned an edge in her voice.

'We could have Room Service up in the suite again.'

Like hell, she thought.

'I'm sorry, Byron, I can't,' she said crisply, almost as though she was turning down a business dinner and not another assignation with her lover.

'Why not?'

'I have things I have to do at home tonight,' she said firmly.

'What? Wash your hair? I'll wash it for you. I'll do anything you want. I'll even paint your toenails if they need painting.'

Celeste groaned silently. What a fool she'd been to surrender her body again to Byron. She should have known what would happen. The man had always been a predator. Now that he was a widower, there was nothing to stop him reverting to type. No guilt. No moral constraints. No nothing.

'I'm having friends for dinner at home,' she said thinking to herself that if Damian brought Gemma home as he said he would then it was close to the truth.

'When are they leaving? I'll come over after they've gone.'

Celeste gritted her teeth. 'Byron, I said no. If you wish to continue to see me then you have to learn to take no for an answer.'

'I'm better at yes,' he growled.

'Aren't we all?'

'When am I going to see you again?'

'I'll call you tomorrow at your office. We'll make plans then.'

'I don't trust you to call. I'll call you.'

'Whatever you like.'

'I'd like to come over later.'

'Byron, for pity's sake!'

'If you had any pity you'd let me come over. God, I think I'm going crazy, Celeste. I can't think of anything else but being with you. You've bewitched me, woman.'

'I'm glad to hear that, Byron. The boot's on the other foot at last.'

She heard his sucked-in breath. 'You're a real bitch, aren't you?'

'So people keep telling me.'

'Add me to the list!' he snarled, and hung up.

Celeste stared down into the dead receiver. Taking a deep, shuddering breath, she hung up herself, then lifted the receiver up again and dialled for a taxi to take her home.

CHAPTER NINE

DAMIAN opened the front door before Celeste could get her key out.

'Hi there, sis. I'm home.'

'So I see,' came her dry reply. 'I take it you're not alone?'

'Hey, why the attitude? You're the one who suggested I bring Gemma here.'

Celeste sighed. 'Maybe I've changed my mind.'

'Too late for that. When you meet her, you'll be glad I did. She's a sweetie.'

'That's what worries me.'

Damian laughed. 'I've been a perfect gentleman.'

'But for how long?'

Damian pulled a face at her, then took her hand and pulled her along to the main living-room where Mrs Nathan Whitmore was curled up in an armchair looking so forlorn that Celeste's heart went out to her.

'Celeste's home at last,' Damian said as they moved into the room.

Gemma jumped, her legs shooting out from under her.

'Don't get up,' Celeste told her, which brought a look of surprise.

Is it my ultra-conservative clothes, Celeste wondered drily, that are making her look at me with those startled doe eyes of hers?

Celeste conceded that with a smart business suit on and her hair up she was a far cry from the outrageously dressed siren who'd attended the Whitmore Opals ball. No doubt this girl thought her as disgraceful a person as her husband did. Not that Nathan could condemn anyone for their morals, or seeming lack of them.

'And how are you bearing up, my dear?' Celeste asked gently. 'I take it things have been a bit difficult for you lately.'

'I ... Yes ... You could say that.'

'Please feel free to stay as long as you like. We have plenty of room here.'

'You're most kind,' the girl murmured. 'Your brother's been very kind too. I ... I don't know what I would have done without him.'

Celeste settled herself in a chair opposite. 'Yes, Damian is not all bad, despite his reputation.'

Now the girl looked even more startled, with Damian quickly coming to his own defence.

'With you for a sister, who needs enemies?' he mocked. 'Don't believe a word she says, Gemma. I'm a saint in wolf's clothing.' He came forward to perch on the arm of her chair, placing a comforting hand on her shoulder.

Gemma looked up at him with a slightly nervous smile, Celeste frowning as she took in how very lovely this child was. Those large velvet-brown eyes were captivating enough, but combined with that flawless olive skin, that sensual mouth and that gloriously thick dark brown hair, she was a stunner. Her attractions did not stop at her face, either. There was no hiding the lush fullness of her breasts beneath that soft green cashmere sweater, the slimline tan stirrup trousers she was wearing just as revealing of the rest of her shapely figure, including the tiny span of her waist and the swell of her quite womanly hips.

'Not to worry, Gemma,' Celeste said briskly. 'I'll keep him in line. And so will Cora. You've told Cora we have an extra for dinner, Damian?'

He gave her a droll look. 'Of course.'

'Maybe you could make yourself scarce for a minute. I have something to say to Gemma.'

'Such as what?'

'If I wanted to tell you, I wouldn't ask you to leave,' she said drily. 'Perhaps you could go select some wine to go with our meal tonight. Gemma looks as if she could do with some relaxing.'

Damian brightened at this suggestion, which only made Celeste more suspicious of his intentions. 'What a good idea! I'll go haunt the cellar. Do you prefer red or white, Gemma?'

'White, actually. Riesling if you have it. Though Nathan always said that ...' She broke off, tears immediately flooding her eyes.

Celeste wanted to kill Nathan Whitmore at that moment. What a bastard! Taking this young girl, making her his then utterly destroying her. She knew exactly what that felt like. Byron had made her irrevocably his in two short weeks. This devil had had months of marriage to brainwash this child both emotionally and sexually.

What chance did she have of throwing off his dastardly influence, of ever being normal with any other man? Celeste recognised the type. This girl felt deeply, as she had felt deeply. No other man would ever do for her, just as no other man but Byron had ever done for Celeste. One only had to look at how she'd acted today, running to him when he'd snapped his fingers, giving him all he asked without asking for anything in return.

His unexpected sympathy today had got to her for a while but, in the end, he'd turned it to his own advantage, using her momentary vulnerability as a springboard to yet another sexual encounter. If ever Celeste needed a recent example of male selfishness, then that would suffice. Or she could gaze upon this crushed creature and her big bruised eyes.

Damn, but she wished she could help her, *really* help her. But she felt so helpless.

'Get lost, Damian,' she bit out, taking his place on the armrest of Gemma's chair and putting a sympathetic arm around her slender shoulders.

'Things might not be as bad as you think, love,' she said softly once Damian had departed. 'I was speaking to Byron today and it seems Nathan insists he's innocent of any wrong-doing with Lenore.'

'Then he's a liar!' the girl bit out heatedly. 'I...I heard him, with my own ears. He...he spent the night with her. And he said other things. Awful things.' She shuddered violently and Celeste wanted to kill Nathan anew. But she had to give this child some hope.

'Sometimes people say things they don't mean to say, Gemma. And they do things they don't mean to do. Men will be men, my dear. Nathan's spending the night with his ex-wife might not be as black and white as it seems. Have—er—things been all they should be between you two in the bedroom lately?'

Celeste could not misinterpret the guilty colour that flooded the girl's cheeks. So! Things hadn't been all hunky-dory between them.

'It had been a couple of weeks since we'd made love,' she admitted unhappily.

'You...you haven't been having an affair with Damian, have you?' she asked carefully.

'No!' There was no doubting the girl's horror at this suggestion. 'I would never do a thing like that. I love Nathan. I always will!' She burst into tears at that, weeping into the crumpled handkerchief in her hands.

'There, there...' Celeste patted her gently on the shoulder. 'Perhaps you should go upstairs, get yourself together, wash your face and then we'll have dinner. I'll walk up with you.'

Celeste kept a comforting arm around her waist as they walked slowly up the stairs together, surprised at the tug of emotion she was feeling for this sweet child. It was not just sympathy. It was a real empathy.

She's so like I was at her age, came the dismaying realisation. Basically innocent and naïve, yet extremely sexual and emotional. Falling in love meant giving of oneself utterly and totally. What a pity the men we fell in love with didn't return the same unfailing devotion.

Celeste resisted telling Gemma that men were not as simple and straightforward as women. She saw no point in making her as cynical and world-weary as she was, nor in explaining to her that a man could sleep with one woman, claiming he loved her, then marry another a few months later. Or that, while married to that woman, he could still lose himself in that first woman's body to such an extent that all reality had ceased to exist, only to turn on her a few minutes later, deriding her most cruelly and banishing her from his life.

Or maybe she should? Maybe it was time the girl heard some of the facts of life.

'How old are you, Gemma?' she asked as they turned at the landing and mounted the rest of the stairs.

'Twenty. I *think*.'

Celeste frowned. 'What do you mean, you think?'

The girl sighed. 'It's a long story. My birth certificate turned out to be full of lies and I'm not sure when my birthday is.'

'How awkward for you.'

Gemma shrugged a type of weary resignation.

'Would you be offended, Gemma,' Celeste asked carefully, 'if I told you that not many husbands go through life being faithful to their wives?'

Those big brown eyes slanted her way, shocking Celeste with their sudden coldness. 'I don't want to be married to that kind.'

Goodness, Celeste thought admiringly. She's not so softly sweet after all. Damian doesn't know what he's in for if he tries anything with this girl.

Celeste found herself feeling much better about that situation. 'I fully agree with you,' she said drily. 'That's why I've never married. What guest room did Damian put you in?'

'That one,' Gemma indicated, pointing ahead to the third door on the right.

'Have you got everything you need?'

'Yes, thank you.'

'Don't bother to change for dinner. You look delightful in what you're wearing. I'm going to slip into something more casual, however. I'll drop back at the door and collect you on my way downstairs.'

'Miss Campbell,' Gemma called after her as she walked away.

Celeste turned, wincing a little. 'Celeste, please. I keep 'Miss Campbell' for junior typists only.'

Gemma smiled, reminding Celeste forcibly of her stunning beauty. 'All right. Celeste. I just wanted to thank you again, and to say that you're not at all like I thought you'd be.'

Celeste smothered an amused smile. 'What did you think I'd be like?'

'I don't know. Not so nice. Oh, that sounds awful!'

'It sounds perfectly reasonable to me. I'm often not very nice, Gemma. But I don't think anyone could help being nice with you.'

Gemma looked disconcerted by this compliment. 'I'm not always so nice, either. Maybe I did push Nathan away from me. I ... I'm not sure of anything any more.' Tears filled her eyes and she looked away.'

Celeste was appalled at the sudden pricking of tears behind her own eyes. Good God, she was going all mushy and sentimental in her old age. It was all Byron's fault, raking up old memories, making her say things she should never have said. Or maybe this unexpected vulnerability was because her own daughter would be about Gemma's age now. She might even look a little like her.

Celeste was not a natural blonde, her fair tresses achieved with considerable effort from her hairdresser. Her daughter was sure to be a brunette, like Gemma, and probably with similar brown eyes. Despite Celeste's own eyes being a light yellowish brown, dark eyes did run in the Campbell family. One only had to look at Damian. Since a blue-eyed father with a brown-eyed mother almost always produced a brown-eyed baby. Celeste's daughter would most likely have deep brown eyes something like Gemma's.

Celeste swallowed and dragged up a covering smile. 'Don't think about it any more tonight,' she advised the obviously confused and very distressed girl. 'I won't be long. I'm a quick dresser.'

Dinner did not prove to be as difficult as Celeste had begun to fear it might be. Damian was his usual charming self and Gemma, with the help of several glasses of wine, relaxed enough to talk a little about herself in a general sense. She explained how Byron had made her learn Japanese before letting her work in any of his stores, and that she'd become quite competent at it.

'You won't have any trouble getting a job, then,' Celeste said. 'There are openings all over the place if you can speak Japanese well.'

'That's what I'm hoping.'

'We could find her a job at Campbell's, couldn't we, Celeste?' Damian suggested casually.

'Any time,' she offered, and meant it. Gemma would be an asset behind any counter.

'I did originally hope that,' the girl admitted. 'But now I think I should strike out on my own. Maybe I'll move interstate.'

'Why in God's name would you do that?' Damian's voice was sharp.

'Because she wants to be independent, Damian,' Celeste explained somewhat caustically. 'A concept I realise you don't understand.'

'She should be near friends at a time like this.'

Gemma gave him an apologetic look. 'I'm sorry. Damian. You've been marvellous, but I really don't like imposing on you and your sister.'

'What rubbish!' they both answered at once, then simultaneously laughed.

'At least stay a week,' Celeste compromised, knowing decisions should not be made in the heat of the moment.

'Yes, give us a week of your delightful company at least,' Damian insisted.

'All right.' Gemma's sigh of acceptance sounded relieved, and Celeste felt another pull on her heart-strings. Damn, in another week she wouldn't want her to go any more than Damian. Despite the traumas surrounding Gemma's visit, it was surprisingly pleasant having her around. Celeste decided she must definitely be entering a sentimental phase in her life. Next thing she'd be getting herself a dog!

'I hear you're an outback girl,' she said by way of changing the subject.

'That's right. Born and bred in Lightning Ridge.'

'Damned awful place!' Damian scorned. 'Hot as hell and wall-to-wall flies. I only went there once. Celeste had this idea about my learning to become an opal buyer. I soon dissuaded her, didn't I?'

'I think I quickly realised that anything with physical discomfort involved was not your forte.'

Gemma laughed. 'Then you wouldn't have wanted to live where I lived. I not only had wall-to-wall flies but wall-to-wall dirt.'

'How's that?' he asked.

'Dad and I lived in a dugout. You know. A hole in the ground. Well, not in the ground exactly. It was dug out of the side of a hill.'

Damian shuddered. 'You poor thing.'

Gemma shrugged. 'I didn't know any differently. But you can imagine what I thought when I came to Sydney and went to live in Belleview. I thought I'd died and gone to heaven.'

'How did that come about, Gemma?' Celeste asked. 'Your going to live at Belleview, that is? Or don't you like my asking that? You don't have to tell us if you don't want.'

'No, it's all right. I don't mind. My dad died, you see. There'd only been the two of us. My mother—er—my mother had died when I was born. I...I decided to come to Sydney to live. To be honest, I never did like the heat and the flies either,' she said with a quick smile Damian's way. 'I decided to sell up everything I inherited to get some money. Not that there was much. Dad was an opal miner, but not a very successful one, I'm afraid. All he had to his name was a battered old truck and a small hoard of second-rate opals. That's why I...why I...'

Her voice trailed away and Celeste suspected some memory was too painful to talk about, for the girl suddenly dropped her eyes to her food and frowned. When she looked up, she still looked troubled for a second then her expression cleared and she resumed her story.

'Anyway, I went to sell these opals to Byron. He goes up to the Ridge to buy opals all the time.'

'Yes, I know,' Celeste said, and threw Damian a reproachful look. 'Byron really knows his opals. So what happened? I hope he gave you a good deal.'

'Well, no, he didn't. I mean he *couldn't*, because he wasn't there. He was in hospital after some accident or other and he'd sent Nathan in his place.'

Celeste nodded thoughtfully. That would have been the boating accident when Irene was killed. 'I see,' she murmured.

And she did. Nathan had taken one look at this exquisite creature and had simply had to possess her.

'So what happened then?' she asked, impatient to see how Nathan had achieved his wicked purpose.

'I sold the opals to Nathan instead.'

'Yes, but how did you come to be living at Belleview?'

'Oh, that. Well, when I mentioned to Nathan that I was moving to Sydney, he gave me his business card and said if I ever needed a job to look him up, so I did.'

'And what job did he offer you that required you to live in at Belleview?' Damian asked, sounding sardonic.

Gemma flushed a little at his obvious innuendo. 'It's not what you're thinking. Nathan offered me a position as sales assistant at one of Whitmore's opal shops, but Byron insisted I learn Japanese first, so while I was doing that Nathan hired me as a type of minder for his daughter. Kirsty was staying with him at Belleview for a while, you see. She'd been giving her mother some trouble and Lenore had sent her to her father to straighten her out. Naturally, I—er—had to live in.'

Celeste almost repeated the *naturally*, but didn't. She did, however, catch Damian's eye across the table and her expression was similarly cynical. Not that he could cast any stones. She'd like a dollar for every devious line he'd thrown a woman.

'And that's when you both fell in love,' Celeste commented matter-of-factly.

'Yes,' Gemma muttered, looking and sounding miserable again.

'Let's talk about something else,' Damian said firmly. 'Some more wine, Gemma?'

She put her hand over the glass and shook her head. 'Any more and I'll be paralytic.'

'At least you'll sleep well.'

Cora came in then, wanting to know who wanted dessert.

'What is it?' Celeste asked.

'Lemon meringue pie with cream.'

Celeste groaned. 'You bad woman, tempting me like that.'

'You shouldn't worry. You can always punish yourself with twenty laps of the pool afterwards.' Cora began stacking up the dinner plates. 'There are no refusals, I take it?'

'No!' they all chorused.

'Just as well,' the housekeeper said crisply. 'I don't like slaving over a hot stove for nothing.'

'She's so nice,' Gemma remarked once Cora was out of earshot.

Damian grinned a wickedly attractive grin. 'We're all nice, aren't we, Celeste?'

She looked at her brother and wished he weren't so handsome, or so charming. Her earlier confidence that Gemma would be able to resist him worried her anew. Women did stupid things on the rebound. Hadn't she gone from Byron to Stefan thinking she could lose herself in his Viking good looks, his supposedly gentlemanly consideration?

And what had happened?

She'd been drawn into a hell that no woman should have to endure but which many did. Celeste could well understand why battered women eventually struck back and did murder. She wished she had had the courage, or the strength. Then she might have kept her lovely baby.

Instead, she'd had her child stolen from her, had been left bleeding and broken on that cold stone floor. If a passing shepherd hadn't heard her pathetic cries for help, she would be dead now. Instead, she had lived to survive. But had her survival been worth it?

Maybe, she decided, looking at Gemma down the end of the table. She could still be of help to people occasionally. And she could still get pleasure out of life occasionally.

Her mind drifted to Byron and she shuddered. Oh, yes, she could still feel pleasure. But when would the pain stop? When would she be able to forget?

CHAPTER TEN

GEMMA sat on the edge of the bed, holding her temples. She shouldn't have drunk so much of that wine. The blood was pounding in her head and she felt a little nauseous. The wine had made her run off at the mouth a little over dinner as well, something she regretted now.

At least she'd stopped herself before she'd told them all about the Heart of Fire. Irrespective of her breakup with Nathan, Gemma felt she owed some loyalty to the Whitmores. Byron had always been good to her and she was sure he wouldn't like her blurting out Whitmore business to the Campbells. Celeste's buying the Heart of Fire at the ball had clearly annoyed Byron. He'd been reluctant to tell her any real details that night of how the opal had come back in Whitmore possession, so one didn't have to be too bright to conclude he wanted to keep that information a secret.

Gemma wasn't too sure why, but since her own father had clearly been involved in the original theft of the opal she didn't mind not telling all and sundry. Celeste and Damian had already been shocked by her less than genteel upbringing at Lightning Ridge. What would they think if she had revealed her father had not only been a drunk and a loser, but a criminal as well?

Not that Celeste Campbell had any right to judge others, Gemma reasoned quickly. Her reputation was hardly lily-white. And yet...

Gemma shook her head, frowning. The scandalous lady boss of Campbell Jewels was not at all as Gemma had imagined her to be. Though clearly an assertive and confident businesswoman who Gemma was sure could be very tough given the right occasion, she also had a sur-

prisingly soft and warm side of her character that was
very engaging. Gemma had found herself drawn to the
woman. She had wanted to pour all her woes out to her,
sensing a genuinely sympathetic ear.

But a lifetime of being a very private person with no
mother, no brothers or sisters and few friends had made
Gemma reluctant to open up to people. Not that Celeste
Campbell could solve her problems. No one could solve
her problems, for there was no solution. She'd fallen in
love with the wrong man, had married him, made him
her life, and now he'd snatched that life out from under
her.

It would be a long, long time before she got over his
betrayal. Maybe a lifetime would not be enough.

A tap on the door had her jumping to her feet. Lord,
but she was a bundle of nerves.

'Yes?' she asked agitatedly through the door.

'I've brought you a nightcap,' Damian returned. 'I
thought you might need one to help you sleep.'

With a sigh, Gemma went over and opened the door to
find Damian standing there with a smile on his handsome face and what looked like a glass of port in his
hands.

'I couldn't possibly drink any more alcohol, Damian,'
she said apologetically. 'But thank you for the thought.'

'You're still dressed,' he chided. 'Look, why don't you
have a relaxing shower, climb into bed and I'll bring you
a mug of hot chocolate?'

'Really, there's no need.'

'There's every need,' he said firmly. 'You should see
the dark rings under your eyes. You need a good night's
sleep, Gemma.'

'All right,' she sighed, agreeing with him. If she didn't
sleep tonight, she wasn't sure what she'd do.

Gemma was under the bedclothes, the sheet pulled well
up over her rather revealing ivory silk nightie—she didn't
have any other kind—when Damian knocked.

Was it her being in bed that made her feel suddenly
vulnerable when he came back in and closed the door
behind him? Or was it the way his flashing black eyes

narrowed on her near naked shoulders as he walked towards her?

Whatever, Gemma found her whole insides contracting, her stomach fluttering with a funny little feeling something like fear. She was not such a fool as to be unaware that Damian fancied her. She'd been rather expecting him to make a pass some time, but she didn't think he'd try something here, with his sister just down the hall.

Still, her eyes followed him somewhat worriedly when he put the drink down on the bedside chest and sat down on the side of the bed. 'Feeling better after your shower?' he asked, smiling.

She nodded, finding it hard to find her tongue all of a sudden.

'I'm an expert at hot-chocolate making,' he said, and picked up the mug again. 'Here... Drink up...'

When he actually held it to her lips instead of handing it to her, she automatically curved her own hands around his, lest the liquid spill on the bed. Appalled to find her fingers trembling, she gulped the drink down very quickly, all the while aware of Damian staring at her over the rim with those penetrating black eyes of his. She found herself staring back at him and seeing him in a totally different light.

Where before he'd presented himself as a darkly elegant and very handsome man with flashing black eyes, a boyish smile and an engagingly charming manner, she now noted a wicked gleam in those eyes and a decadent weakness in the slack set of his mouth. Dressed all in black as he was tonight, and with his straight black hair slicked back from his face, he gave off a menacing aura that was making her heart beat faster and her stomach churn. All she wanted was for him to leave her room as soon as possible.

'All gone,' she said with false brightness once she'd drunk all the hot chocolate and was able to take her hands away from his.

'Good girl. Sleep well, now.'

Gemma could not help her look of surprise when he simply stood up and began to walk towards the door.

She was still staring at him when he stopped with his hand on the doorknob and looked back over his shoulder. 'I suggest you sleep in as long as you can tomorrow morning. Unfortunately, I have to show my face in the office, but Cora will be here all day to look after you. Feel free to use the pool—it's heated—or anything else that appeals, and I'll see you when I get home tomorrow evening. OK?'

His smile was so warm and tender that she felt guilty at her earlier bad thoughts about him. Her imagination was definitely getting the better of her. Or maybe her opinion of men had been seriously damaged by what Nathan had done.

'I'll never forget how sweet you've been to me,' she said with genuine feeling. 'I don't know what I would have done without you.'

'Men can be good friends too, Gemma. Always remember that.'

'I will from now on.'

IT WAS AFTER two when Damian slipped back into her room. The sleeping tablets he'd crushed in her drink would be at their peak now. He'd tripled the normal dose, making sure of her unconscious state.

The room was in darkness, the curtains drawn at the windows. Making his way carefully over to them, he very slowly drew them back so that moonlight fell across the bed and the sleeping form within.

Standing next to the bed, he gazed down at her for ages then very slowly peeled the bedclothes back down. Shock riveted him to the spot when she moaned and rolled over on to her side, facing him. But her eyes remained shut, her lips softly apart as she breathed the deep, even breathing of the heavily drugged. His own eyes fell to where her movement had wrapped the nightie tightly around her body, the top awry on her full bosom.

His gut clenched down hard at the sight of half a rosy nipple peeping out at him, his desire flaring madly. The

idea of touching her while she was asleep was so exciting
that he actually shuddered.

He recalled how her hands had trembled on his earlier
tonight. She'd been momentarily afraid of him till he'd
managed to allay her fears with his wimpish retreat. But
she had every reason to be afraid of him, though, didn't
she? Every reason...

His own hands trembled as he reached out to draw the
strap down off her shoulder and down her arm. He was
about to expose her breast totally when he heard the
sound of the doorknob turning. Reefing the strap back
up, he dived under the bed and was hiding there, quivering, when he saw his sister's slippers appear beside the
bed.

Holding his breath lest she hear his breathing, he listened to her rearranging the bedclothes, then watched her
walk over to the windows where she drew the curtains,
blessedly darkening that side of the room. His relief when
she left the room was enormous, but for some rotten
reason Celeste left the damned door ajar. And the light
in the hall was on.

Clearly, his sister was having one of her sleepless
nights, when she would wander the house at all hours. If
he closed the door, she might see it.

Damian lay where he was for some time before slipping out from under the bed and returning to his room.
Though furious, he put his frustration on hold with the
thought that tomorrow was another day. He determined
that it would not only be Gemma's drink he put the
sleeping draught in the next time. Darling Celeste was
going to have her insomnia fixed as well.

GEMMA WOKE with a terrible hangover. She groaned
when she saw the time. Nearly noon. How could she have
slept for so long?

Dragging herself out of bed, she visited the *en suite*
then returned to draw on her only modest dressing-
gown—a floor-length cream silk number whose cover-
age was adequate, although it wasn't the thickest of
material. Still, only Cora would be left in the house at this
late hour. Damian and Celeste would have gone to work.

Work...

Gemma felt guilty about how she'd let her own work-mates down yesterday, ringing up at the last moment and claiming she was sick. She would have to ring again to-day and let them know the real situation, though maybe Byron had already done that. From what Celeste said last night, her father-in-law already knew everything.

Picking up her hairbrush, she began putting some or-der into her tangled hair. She really had had a restless night, despite sleeping so long. There was a vague mem-ory of dreams which she was rather glad she could not remember. She was sure they hadn't been happy dreams. But they weren't likely to be, were they?

With her appearance in some semblance of order, she went in search of Cora and a cup of coffee. Maybe some aspirin as well. She really did not feel too good. Her head was terribly thick. Not exactly a headache but a woolly feeling.

Gemma glanced admiringly around on her way down-stairs, especially at the elaborate stained-glass window rising above the landing halfway down. Her stark out-back upbringing made her appreciate beautiful things but she was not naïve enough to think that riches brought happiness. Her own marriage to a wealthy successful man certainly proved the saying that money wasn't every-thing. It was *nothing* if not combined with love and true intimacy. Nathan had showered her with clothes and gifts, given her everything but himself in a real sense. She'd been worried all along by their lack of emotional bonding, worried Nathan's feelings for her didn't go deeper than lust and possessiveness, and she'd been proven right.

Gemma stepped off the staircase with a sigh and headed for the kitchen, looking in the other rooms on the way.

The kitchen was empty, and there, on the counter, propped against a bowl of fruit, was a note.

Gone to do the week's shopping. I've put a selection of cereals on the side. Coffee and tea next to them. There's milk and orange juice in the fridge, bread al-

ready in the toaster. Help yourself. Be back by three.
Cora.

'Just coffee to start with, Cora,' Gemma told the absent housekeeper. 'Pity about the aspirin.'

She took the steaming mug back upstairs with her, sipping down most of it before stripping off and plunging into the shower, in the hope that the hot jets of water would clear her head. No such luck. She really needed a couple of painkillers.

Unfortunately, the wall cabinet in the guest *en suite* was empty apart from a spare toothbrush, some mouthwash, and a couple of tubes of toothpaste. Gemma didn't think anyone would mind if she searched the other medicine cabinets for something to take, so she covered her nakedness with her robe and walked out of her bedroom into the next.

Clearly, it was a man's bedroom, the furniture dark, the brown and gold furnishings having not a single piece of feminine frippery about any of them. There was also an absence of the type of ornament and knick-knack women dotted around their rooms. The bed was made and the room tidy, but the black trousers and shirt Damian had worn the previous evening were draped across a chair in the corner.

Not wanting to linger, Gemma hurried across the room and into the connecting bathroom. This time, the cabinet was full of a wide range of medicine and other items, including several packets of condoms. Gemma tried not to make judgement over this—at least he was practising safe sex—but seeing so many of them sitting there so openly and so casually sent a funny little shiver down her spine. Her eyes darted along the shelves and when she spied some headache tablets she snatched them up, extracted a couple and put the packet back, relieved to slide the glass door back into place. Popping them into her mouth, she turned on the tap, cupped her hands and drank from the pool of water that formed in them.

When she lifted her head from this action and automatically glanced in the mirror, she screamed.

For Nathan was standing in the open bedroom doorway, glaring over at her as though he wanted to kill her.

She whirled round, and her eyes had never felt bigger
as they took in his unshaven face and his chillingly cold
grey eyes. Dressed in washed-out grey jeans and a crumpled blue windcheater, he looked far removed from his
usual elegant, well-groomed self. He looked far removed from his usual self all round. Dear God, he had
never looked at her like that before, so full of hardness
and hatred.

After an initial freezing, Gemma's heart jolted into an
erratic beat, her headache forgotten in the face of other
more frightening feelings.

'So I was right,' he said in a voice made all the more
terrifying for its control. 'You were here all along. I just
jumped to the wrong conclusion.'

Gemma pulled the robe defensively around her quivering nudity. 'How...how did you get in here? The gates
are locked.'

'There's no lock on the jetty, Gemma. I came by boat.'

'I'm not alone, you know,' she bluffed, sensing his
simmering violence. 'The housekeeper...'

'Won't be back till three,' he finished frostily, and
produced Cora's note from his pocket. Crumpling it into
a ball, he threw it in a corner. 'I came here,' he ground
out, 'hoping and praying that somehow I'd be proven
wrong about you, that all I had to do to set things right
was say I was sorry for being so stupid as to have Lenore
over. But I wasn't wrong about you, was I? You took the
first flimsy excuse you could find to run to your lover.
You blackened my name to my whole family while all the
time you were letting that bastard Campbell screw you
silly!'

Gemma hadn't realised till that moment what impression her presence in Damian's room would give, especially with her not being properly dressed. Any irony over
Nathan's turning things around and making her the ac-
cused one was lost in the wake of her anxiety to make him
see the truth.

'You've got it all wrong!' she defended. But in vain, she thought. There was no reasoning in Nathan's face. No capacity to listen. Yet she had to try. Having him believe such a thing of her was untenable. 'I...I only came in here to get some aspirin. Here...look!' She slid back the cabinet and pointed to the packet of tablets.

Nathan's chilling gaze moved from the aspirin to the other packets on the shelf, then returned to survey Gemma's swiftly flushing face with a chillingly mocking expression.

Oh, why do I have to look so guilty? Gemma agonised.

'I know what you're thinking but you're wrong!' she cried. 'There's nothing between Damian and myself. I'm staying here as a guest,' she explained desperately, 'and I have my own room. I'll show it to you. It has my things in it.'

When she hurried forward and went to brush past him, Nathan grabbed both her arms and swung them behind her, holding her wrists in an iron grip while he pushed her back into Damian's room. He slammed her face-down on to the bed, his breathing ragged behind her.

'You might have your own room but *this* is where you've been spending your nights, you lying, cheating bitch! I've known it from the moment that hotel clerk described to me the man who came to collect you. You've been seeing Damian Campbell ever since that night of the ball, haven't you?'

'No!' she cried, terrified now. 'I swear to you, I haven't. 'I...I did run into him one day, but we...we only had coffee.'

Nathan laughed. 'Damian doesn't just have coffee with women, Gemma. He doesn't *just* have anything. The man's well known for his perversions. One in particular.'

Gemma was horrified when she felt her robe being pushed up to her waist, exposing her bare buttocks.

'It seems you haven't progressed to that yet,' he muttered darkly. 'But you will. And he's welcome to you. You know, I sometimes wondered when you would change, when you would fall 'out of love'. I always knew you were far too young for true love. And far, far too beautiful. Extremely beautiful women rarely love. They're too bloody self-centered!'

'I do so love you,' she sobbed.

'Do you?' he jeered. 'Do you really? In that case you won't mind if I have a little of what you've been denying me these last couple of weeks.'

Gemma gasped when she felt him cruelly enclose her two wrists in one brutal grasp on the small of her back, when she heard the sound of his opening his trousers. He jammed a knee between her thighs, forcing them apart.

'Oh, God . . . no, don't . . . don't do this, Nathan!'

But it was already happening before she'd finished her plea. Disbelief brought a type of horrified submission, his harsh panting echoing in her ears. When he finally ejaculated and withdrew, she just lay there, stunned. Silent tears began to stream down her cheeks and she couldn't bear to turn over and look at him.

She vaguely heard him mutter something, heard him rearrange his clothing. Stiffly she closed her legs and buried her face in the quilt. When he laid a perversely gentle hand on her shoulder, she shuddered, and his hand retreated.

'I'm sorry,' he said in the most hollow-sounding voice. 'God . . .'

There was the sound of footsteps gradually receding and then there was an awful silence. It was ages before Gemma could bring herself to move, creeping back off the bed and running back to her bathroom where she turned on the shower and climbed in despite still having the robe on. The water gushed over her, soothing, cleaning water. But she couldn't seem to get herself clean. No matter what she did, she felt dirty and unclean and ugly.

In the end she had to get out of the shower before she turned red-raw. Fresh underwear and a soft flannel tracksuit went some way to making her feel better in a physical sense but she suspected that emotionally and mentally she was walking a razor's edge. If only she had

a mother to confide in, someone who loved her unconditionally, who really cared what happened to her.

The image of Celeste's sympathetic face last night
came to mind. While she was hardly a mother figure, she
was a woman of the world. She would understand what
had happened here today, would perhaps help her put it
into perspective. One part of Gemma almost understood Nathan's reaction to finding her in Damian's bedroom. Another part was so outraged she couldn't bear to
think about it. On top of everything else, she'd begun to
doubt what she had heard with her own ears in their
apartment the other day.

Nathan had acted the wronged husband with such vehemence! Could she be wrong? Had she misheard something? How could she have? What Lenore and Nathan
had said to each other was crystal-clear, and so utterly,
utterly damning. There could be no excuse. No explanation.

And yet . . .

Gemma forced herself to return to Damian's bedroom
to check that she had left no evidence behind of what had
transpired there. For a long moment, she stood in the
doorway, staring at the indentation in the bed. Luckily,
there was no stain, but still, she felt sick just looking at
it. She would never forgive Nathan. Never!

She raced over and plumped up the mattress, straight-
ening the quilt with sweeping strokes, her colour and
emotions high.

How dared he speak so disparagingly of Damian? she
thought agitatedly. Perverse, indeed! The man was a saint
compared to Nathan. A misunderstood and genuinely
kind man. The only pervert in this house today was her
husband. No, *ex*-husband. She couldn't divorce him
quickly enough. If she felt she could make the charge
stick, she would have him charged with rape. Men should
not be allowed to get away with treating their wives like
that!

But Gemma was wise enough these days to know she
had no hope of getting a conviction. It was a man's world
all right, she thought bitterly.

As she turned to leave the room, Cora's crumpled note in the corner caught Gemma's eye. Swooping on it, she stuffed it in her pocket and hurriedly left the room. She couldn't stay here any longer, she decided. She would talk to Celeste when she got home tonight, ask her for a job at one of her interstate stores and make the move as soon as possible.

With this thought in mind, she went back into her room and packed, leaving nothing out but her night-wear and toiletries. She was coming back downstairs to put her soaked robe out on the clothes line when Cora came home.

Gemma schooled her face into a blank mask, surprising herself when she was able to conduct a normal conversation with Cora as the other woman went about preparing the evening meal. So it came as a considerable shock when Celeste and Damian came home, Gemma immediately found her iron composure crumbling. When Damian disappeared upstairs to change and Gemma found herself briefly alone with Celeste in the living-room, she promptly burst into tears.

CHAPTER ELEVEN

CELESTE was stunned.

Gemma had seemed happy enough when they'd arrived home, yet suddenly, here she was, in floods of tears. All she could think to do was to hold her. At first the action felt awkward, but when the girl dropped her head on to her shoulder with a shuddering sigh, the most amazing wave of maternal love swept through Celeste and she found herself embracing Gemma quite naturally and without embarrassment.

'You poor darling,' she murmured, holding her close and stroking her back. 'It's Nathan again, isn't it?'

'He . . . he was here today,' she choked out.

Celeste pulled back in shock. '*Here*? In this *house*?'

Gemma nodded, her misery obvious.

'But how? I mean . . . you must have let him in.'

She shook her head in vigorous denial. 'He said he came by boat. He . . . he just appeared upstairs. I nearly died.'

'Where was Cora?'

'Shopping.'

'Oh, yes, it's Wednesday. She always does the grocery shopping on Wednesday. So what did he do?'

Celeste was appalled when the girl looked stricken and then blushed. *Blushed*, mind you.

The awful reality came to Celeste in a rush and she almost vomited on the spot, gagging down her revulsion with great difficulty. 'He raped you, didn't he?' she said, her voice shaking.

The girl stared at her, making Celeste aware that she must have been looking very peculiar. 'He . . . he didn't beat you, did he?'

The girl looked horrified. 'Oh, no! Nathan wouldn't do a thing like that!'

Celeste pulled herself together but she still couldn't quite get a grasp of the situation. Why was she defending this monster? He should be hung, drawn and quartered!

'He was upset because he found me in Damian's bathroom,' Gemma explained shakily. 'I'd just had a shower and had gone in there to find some aspirin. I...I only had a thin robe on. He thought Damian and I had been having an affair, even before I left him. He was...most upset.'

'Which gave him the right to *rape* you?' Celeste gaped in disbelief.

'Of course not,' Gemma countered. 'But I can see now that there were mitigating circumstances leading to the incident.'

'The incident,' Celeste repeated weakly. Dear God...

She stood there, incredibly shaken, till gradually her tottering emotions came together with a vengeance.

'He must pay,' she bit out. 'He can't be allowed to get away with this.'

Gemma shook her head. 'I thought that at first but my wish for revenge, or justice if you will, is beginning to weaken. No judge or jury would convict him anyway. Besides, there's nothing to be gained by locking Nathan up. He's not really a criminal. He's no danger to society or even to me. I'm sure he'll never do again what he did today. It's not as though he even hurt me physically. There's not a mark on me.'

'There is on your *mind*! Celeste protested.

'My mind is quite clear now,' Gemma insisted with such conviction that Celeste was staggered. 'It is Nathan's mind which will be affected by what transpired here today. I think it will live with him for a long, long time. He's not some brute or monster, Celeste. Underneath that cool façade he wears, he's a very vulnerable human being, but I think he's very mixed up when it comes to his concept of love. I don't think he knows what love is. I don't think he ever did...'

'My God, you still love him, don't you?' Celeste said.

Gemma's smile was so sad that Celeste almost burst into tears herself. 'I will always love him,' the girl admitted.

Celeste stood there, shaking her head and feeling hopelessly confused—till she remembered her own incredible weakness in still loving Byron. How could she sit in judgement when she was guilty of the same blind stupidity?

'I can't stay here any longer, Celeste,' Gemma said simply but firmly. 'I'm extremely grateful for all you and Damian have done for me but I think it best if I got right away, away from Nathan and Sydney. Much as I'm quite sure Nathan won't assault me again, he might make a nuisance of himself. I'm all packed,' she went on with a down-to-earth bravery Celeste could only admire. 'I'll call a taxi after dinner and go to the airport Hilton. I've already called them and booked a room. And I've booked a ticket on a flight back to Lightning Ridge tomorrow.'

'But you said you hated it there.'

'It's where my roots are. And there's something unfinished there that I have to finish to my satisfaction before I can even think of going on with my life.'

'What? What do you have to finish?'

'I'm sorry but I'd rather not discuss that. It's very private and quite painful to me. I think if I started talking about it tonight I'd really break down. So please, don't press me about it.'

'I wouldn't dream of it, my dear. I just wanted to help, that's all. You must know how very fond of you I've grown, even in this short time we've had you here.'

The girl's smile was so sweet that Celeste again struggled to contain her emotions. 'I've grown very fond of you too. And Damian's the best friend I've ever had. He had almost single-handedly restored my faith in the opposite sex.'

Celeste remained diplomatically silent on this score. If there was one plus about Gemma moving out it would be that she wouldn't have to keep feeling uneasy about

Damian's intentions. 'I—er—I think it might be wise to keep your immediate destination a secret from Damian though, don't you? The fewer people who know, the better.'

'What? Oh . . . all right. But what will I tell him?'

'Nothing. I'll tell him after you're gone that I've sent you away on a little holiday. A cruise, perhaps, so that he can't even *think* of following you.'

The girl looked startled, then slightly worried. 'You think he might try to follow me?'

'I think,' Celeste said drily, 'that Damian might want eventually to deepen your friendship into something else. You're a lovely-looking girl, Gemma, and not nearly as naïve as I originally thought. Don't disappoint me by underestimating your attractions, or Damian's weakness for beautiful women.'

Those big brown eyes widened before becoming steady and thoughtful. 'I won't, Celeste. Thank you for speaking plainly. I appreciate it.'

'I have a reputation for speaking plainly.' She smiled a wry, lop-sided smile. 'I have a reputation for a lot of things!'

'None of them deserved, I'm sure. You're a good person. I won't believe any of that horrible gossip about you any more.'

Celeste kept smiling even while her heart flipped over. 'A girl of rare judgement.'

'You can't fool someone from the bush. Or children. Or dogs. Dogs always know a good person when they see one.'

There was a rueful note in Gemma's voice that piqued Celeste's curiosity. But it didn't seem the right moment to question her. Maybe one day, they'd have the chance to have a real heart-to-heart. Celeste knew she would like that. Very much.

'What are you going to do after you settle whatever you have to settle in Lightning Ridge?'

'I'm not sure. That will depend on how things pan out.'

'Will you promise to keep in touch, let me know what you decide to do with your life when you do decide?'

'You really want me to?'

'Of course!'

Her smile was dazzling. 'Then I will be happy to.'

'Good. Now I must pop upstairs and get into my swimming costume. I've been very naughty this week, not keeping up my exercise routine. Care to join me in the pool?'

'I'll come with you and watch, if you like, but I don't feel much like swimming.'

'All right. Why don't you stay here and watch TV while I change and I'll pick you up on the way through?'

Celeste was hurrying along the hall and had one foot on the bottom step when the telephone rang. Instant intuition warned her to take the call.

'I'll get that, Cora!' she called out and bolted down the end of the hall to pick up the receiver. 'Yes?' she said rather breathlessly.

'Is that you, Celeste?'

Her breath caught. Byron. It was Byron, ringing her. She hadn't heard from him since he'd hung up the previous afternoon, and she'd had too much pride to contact him. But with the sound of his voice, her heart had stopped for a moment, only to pulse back to life with a galloping rate. Dear lord, this was definitely getting out of hand, but how was she to stop herself? Her feelings for Byron had never responded to logic or common sense or even pride. They had the impetus of a runaway rollercoaster and about as much stopability.

'Yes,' she said, sounding like a schoolgirl who'd just been telephoned by the captain of the football team. 'It's me.'

'Would you be able to come over here this evening after dinner?' he asked abruptly.

'To Belleview?' she was shocked. She hadn't been invited into those hollowed walls since . . .

Any feelings of excitement or pleasurable anticipation were immediately tainted by dark memories from the past. Belleview was the last place she would choose to be with Byron.

Still, if he wanted her to go there, if he wanted her as much as she was instantly wanting him, then she simply had to go.

'That's right,' he said curtly. 'And I want you to bring Gemma.'

These last words flicked a stinging rebuke across Celeste's silly heart. Her presumption that Byron had rung to organise a romantic rendezvous had been premature, and typically female. After witnessing Gemma's blind love for Nathan, she was extra-sensitive to her own stupidity regarding this man who had done nothing but hurt her.

'And why should I do that?' she lashed out. 'If you want to see Gemma, then come here.'

'That won't work, I'm afraid. I have no way of contacting Lenore back. And she's coming here.'

'What's Lenore got to do with this?' Celeste demanded, though she had a feeling she already knew. The bitch was going to deliver a whole lot of lies to whitewash Nathan.

'Lenore thinks she knows what Gemma overheard between Nathan and herself the other day. She said it would have sounded bad but is perfectly explainable.'

'Is that so?'

'She only just found out this afternoon what happened between Gemma and Nathan. Apparently, Nathan's totally shattered. Can't work. Can't do anything.'

'I'm so sorry for him,' Celeste's words dripped with an acid sarcasm.

Byron sighed. 'I do realise a man would never get your sympathy, Celeste, but we do have feelings too, you know.'

'Only below the waist.' It was on the tip of her tongue to tell Byron what that appalling boy he'd so nobly adopted had done to his wife this afternoon, but she bit her tongue. Gemma's amazing understanding of that bastard's vile actions meant she was sure to want to keep the 'incident' a secret. Celeste herself could not imagine such understanding, but she had to admire the girl for her stance and would not dream of betraying her trust simply to gain a petty victory over Byron.

'Well, are you coming or not?' Byron asked curtly. 'I would suggest you send Gemma over in a taxi but I don't have any faith in her turning up.'

'You honestly expect me to bring that poor child over to have a face-to-face meeting with a lying adulterous whore?'

'People in glass houses shouldn't throw stones, Celeste,' Byron bit out.

'I do not sleep with married men,' Celeste snapped before she realised what she'd said.

'You mean not any more, don't you?' came the inevitable remark, delivered in a bitterly cutting tone.

'That's right.'

'How very fortunate that I'm widowed, then. I wouldn't like to be the one to spoil your wonderful moral standards. But we digress,' he went on with crushing coolness. 'Will you bring Gemma here or not? I suppose I could always wait till Lenore arrives and bring her over there, but that's a lot of time wasted, isn't it?'

'When do you expect her?' Celeste asked sharply.

'Around nine.'

'I don't drive these days. I'll have to take a taxi.'

'Gemma can drive. And she knows the way. Do you have a car she can use?'

Celeste thought of Damian's Ferrari and dismissed it. And the Rolls was too big. 'We'll come in a taxi,' she decided aloud.

'Whatever you prefer. Just come. It's important.'

'Oh, I'll come, Byron. I wouldn't miss the chance of seeing you again.'

'There won't be any of that tonight, Celeste. And definitely not here.'

'We'll see, Byron. We'll see.'

Celeste hung up, aware that she was shaking. That man, she decided angrily, needed taking down a peg or two. He also needed a salutary lesson on who was run-

ning this affair. Did he honestly think he could control his
desire for her any more than she could control hers for
him? If she wanted Byron to make love to her tonight—
at Belleview or any other damned place—then that was
what was going to happen.

Muttering her frustrations to herself, she was about to
flounce off back down the hall when the reason for
Byron's call in the first place flooded back into her mind.
Her groan was full of guilt and dismay. What was the
matter with her? God, but she was a selfish bitch.

A severe mental lecture followed, after which she
forced her thinking processes back on to the serious
matter at hand: Gemma's happiness. What if Lenore
could genuinely whitewash what Gemma had heard or
seen that day? What then? Would she go back to that
bastard? Celeste did not feel at all confident that she
wouldn't.

But I suppose that's up to her, she realised with a resigned sigh. We all have to do what we have to do. And
how can I sit in judgement? When it comes to matters of
love, I've made the biggest mess of my life. I'm still
making the biggest mess of my life!

Love, she thought savagely, has a lot to answer for!

Gathering herself, Celeste strode back down the hall
and into the living-room, knowing in her heart that she
wouldn't have much trouble convincing Gemma to go
with her to Belleview. That girl was as much in love as *she*
was. Which meant she was doomed to make stupid decisions and do stupid things!

CHAPTER TWELVE

'I REALLY will have to start driving again,' Celeste muttered under her breath when the taxi lurched into the adjacent lane and accelerated with hair-raising speed up the next hill, only to have to brake madly when the lights ahead changed to red.

It had begun to drizzle as they left Campbell Court and the roads were becoming dangerously slick. When the lights turned green and the driver screeched off, she leant forward and tapped him on the shoulder. 'We'd like to get where we're going in one piece, if you don't mind.'

'Sure thing, lady.' He grinned at her in the rear-view mirror, without changing his speed one iota.

Celeste sighed and sank backwards.

Gemma gave her a weak smile. 'We'll be there soon,' she whispered.

'And none too soon.'

In an attempt not to have her heart jump right into her mouth every few seconds, Celeste tipped her head back, closed her eyes and tried to think of other things.

Damian had not been too thrilled with her news that she was taking Gemma out to meet with Lenore after dinner. When she refused to explain further, he'd said some very rude things, then stormed out of the house and taken off in his Ferrari. Celeste felt a little badly about this—and so did Gemma—but at least it stopped any awkward questions over why Gemma had to take two suitcases with her just to see Lenore. The conditional plan was for her to go on to the airport Hilton after Celeste had been dropped home.

'Did Byron give you any idea what Lenore's supposed explanation is?' Gemma asked as the taxi slowed to turn into Belleview.

Celeste opened her eyes and straightened. 'No. Sorry.' She was surprised at how agitated just seeing the house was making her. There were too many bad memories here. And yet it was a beautiful home. Elegant and graceful. Like one of those great Southern mansions.

Maybe it wasn't the house that was agitating her. Maybe it was the way she was dressed.

Celeste cringed a little when she imagined the expression on Byron's face when he saw her. But damn it all, she had to get something out of this meeting other than high blood-pressure and a sleepless night.

'That's Lenore's car,' Gemma informed her as the taxi pulled in behind a small sedan.

Celeste brushed aside Gemma's offer to pay for the taxi, relieved to be out of the potential coffin, even if she was no longer looking forward to the coming encounter with Byron.

'Put the luggage up there beside the door,' she ordered the driver, after which she gave him a generous note and happily dismissed him. The thought that she would have to take a taxi all that way home again in the rain did not sit well with her, but she decided to worry about that later. Her immediate concern was keeping her cool and her wits about her. Suddenly, she wasn't so sure what Byron's reaction to her appearance would be and she wanted to be ready for any outcome.

Both women mounted the steps that led up to the white-columned portico and the massive front doors. Celeste leant against the doorbell, throwing Gemma a reassuring look as they waited to be let in.

'You look fine,' she said when Gemma started nervously brushing down her clothes. The combination of a cream woolen trouser suit with a caramel silk shirt underneath was both sophisticated and flattering on her tall shapely figure, yet Celeste gained the impression that the girl did not feel confident in her clothes. Why was that?

she wondered. The reflection Gemma saw when she looked in the mirror had to please her.

Her own reflection was something else. Celeste had poured herself into some scandalously tight jeans for the occasion. Add to these a black lace bodysuit, black ankle-height boots with stiletto heels, and a black leather battle jacket, and you had a dangerously provocative image. With her hair piled haphazardly on top of her head, gold gypsy hoops dangling from her lobes, she looked like a refugee from a bikers' meeting.

Or Cher gone blonde.

Byron answered the door, and his face betrayed not a single darned thing when those piercing blue eyes of his briefly raked over her. Gemma, however, received a warm greeting and a solicitous hand, while Celeste was totally ignored. When Byron drew Gemma inside she had no option but to trail after them or stay standing where she was like a shag on a rock.

'Aren't you coming in?' Byron was forced to ask when he went to shut the door.

'Not till you've said hello and invited me in.'

His smile sent a prickle running down her spine. My God, he hates me, she realised. Hates whatever power I have over him. Hates what I can make him feel.

Good, she thought savagely, and waited.

'Hello, Celeste,' he said with icy politeness. 'Do come in.'

By this time Gemma was looking perturbed behind Byron. Celeste decided not to make a scene, brushing past Byron to walk into the spider's parlour. But *she* would remain the spider, she decided fiercely. And *he* would stay the fly.

'Can I take your coat?' he asked with false gallantry.

'I'll keep it on, thanks,' she countered. 'It's chilly in here. Must be all the marble. Is Ava home? I'd like to see this miraculous transformation you told me about.'

'What transformation?' Gemma asked, frowning.

'Ava's lost a lot of weight lately,' Byron explained. 'Smartened herself up no end. Sorry, Celeste, but she's not home. She's out with her fiancé.'

'*Fiancé*!' Gemma gasped. 'Ava's *engaged*?'

'She is indeed. To a charming Italian man by the name of Vince Morelli.'

'Good heavens, when did all this happen?'

'Just this past weekend.'

Gemma's smile faded suddenly. 'A lot of things happened this past weekend...'

'Apparently,' Byron muttered. 'Which is why I asked Celeste to bring you here. We're about to sort one of them out. Lenore's waiting for us in the family-room. Shall we?' He waved the two women on ahead. When Gemma looked reluctant to move, Celeste took her elbow and guided her down the corridor past the grandfather clock.

Lenore was sitting on one of the huge leather sofas that dominated the large casually furnished room, looking so intimidatingly chic in black silk culottes and a crisp white blouse, her glorious red hair twisted into an elegant French roll, that Celeste had a sudden insight into Gemma's unexpected attack of insecurity outside the front door.

Nathan's first wife made her feel inadequate and inferior. It was the old *Rebecca* syndrome, understandable given the gap in their ages, not to mention the enormous gap in their relative life experiences. What a pity Gemma didn't understand that it was these very differences that had probably attracted Nathan to her in the first place.

'Hello, Lenore,' Gemma said stiffly.

Celeste watched Lenore like a hawk. There was no doubting she was giving a marvellous performance as the halting and embarrassed 'other woman' as she stood up, went to come forward, then stayed where she was.

'This is even worse than I thought it would be,' she said with just the right amount of dismay. 'I mean...I do see that I might have been insensitive to your feelings, Gemma, taking far too much of Nathan's time. But you have to believe me when I say there has been nothing of a sexual nature between us since our divorce.'

'That's a lie,' Gemma said in a low, shaking voice. 'Even if I somehow made a mistake on Sunday—though

I don't see how—I saw you and Nathan kissing one night in this very house!'

Was that sincere astonishment on the woman's face? Celeste wondered. Or more brilliant acting!

'It was in the billiard-room,' Gemma added bitingly. 'The very first night I came to stay.'

Lenore seemed to recall something but her glance Gemma's way was full of pity. 'Dear girl, that was nothing.'

'Don't patronise me,' Gemma lashed out. 'The kiss I saw was not *nothing*!'

Lenore had the good grace to blush. 'Maybe not nothing,' she admitted unhappily, 'but it was nothing for you to worry about.'

'I hate to interupt,' Byron said carefully. 'But a kiss all those months ago is not what Lenore has graciously come here to explain. Please, Gemma, let's try to keep some perspective in all this. At that time, you hardly knew Nathan. Or am I wrong about that?' he queried softly.

Celeste blinked when Gemma sliced an icy look Byron's way. This girl could really take care of herself! For some unaccountable reason, she felt a fierce pride. It must be a sisterhood empathy, she reasoned after a momentary confusion. But truly, this girl kept evoking feelings in her that she'd never felt before.

'There was nothing between Nathan and myself when I came to live here,' she returned firmly.

'And there was nothing between Nathan and myself last weekend,' Lenore insisted.

'How can you possibly say that?' Gemma attacked, her face flushing with anger and outrage. 'I heard you myself and I could not misinterpret what I heard.'

'What exactly did you hear?' Lenore asked, looking not at all like a guilty party, merely a concerned one.

Celeste was totally perplexed.

Gemma was staring at Lenore as well. 'You want me to repeat it in front of others?'

'Word for word.'

'Word for word!'

'Yes.'

'Oh...I...I'm not sure I can remember it all word for word.'

'*Try*. What was the first thing you heard? Who was speaking?'

'It...it was Nathan. He said...he said... "So what if it was just sex between us last night? When has it ever been anything else?" And you said... "When has it ever been anything else but sex for you with any woman?" And then Nathan laughed.'

'What a bastard,' Celeste muttered.

'Shut up,' Byron hissed from where he'd moved to be standing right behind her shoulder.

'What next?' Lenore probed mercilessly and Gemma winced.

Celeste couldn't stand the pain in those lovely brown eyes any longer. 'For pity's sake, Byron,' she whispered, throwing him a desperate look.

'Patience,' he exhorted under his breath.

Gemma was clearly struggling to remember the exact words. 'I think you then said something about having been in love with him when you got pregnant with Kirsty...'

'Would the words have been... "You think I didn't love you that night all those years ago, when we made a baby together? You think that was only sex for me?"'

Gemma was taken aback. 'Yes, that's it. That's it exactly! Nathan replied he knew it was only sex and you called him a bastard.'

With a shuddering sigh, Lenore bent and picked up a large plastic folder from the coffee-table in front of her. Opening it, she flipped over some of the printed pages within, then brought it over to show Gemma, pointing to a spot at the beginning of one of the pages. 'Read from here,' she instructed.

Celeste watched as all the blood drained from Gemma's face. When she finally did look up, her cheeks were ashen and there were tears in her eyes. 'It's all from Nathan's play,' she choked out. 'Everything I heard was words from Nathan's play...'

'It's a scene I've been having trouble with,' Lenore explained. 'Nathan kept saying I wasn't putting enough emotion into it. He...he was helping me with it on Sunday, playing the part of my leading man.'

'Oh, God,' Gemma groaned, swaying on her feet.

Celeste rushed forward and grabbed her, making her sit down. 'Some brandy, Byron,' she ordered. 'Or some whisky. *Quickly*!'

'Won't be a sec,' he bit out, and hurried from the room.

'Oh, Celeste,' Gemma cried brokenly. 'What have I done?'

'Surely things can be fixed up between you and Nathan now that you know the truth,' Lenore suggested, in total ignorance of what had transpired that afternoon.

Celeste shook her head. 'You don't understand.'

'I'll speak to Nathan myself,' Lenore offered.

Byron returned to give Celeste a glass with a hefty slug of brandy in it which she proceeded to force a distraught Gemma to drink.

'I think, Lenore,' Byron said, 'that it's best if *I* speak to Nathan. Do you know where he is tonight?'

'Not really. We were to have a full dress rehearsal for the play today but he didn't turn up. We went ahead anyway and he did make an appearance towards the end of it in the most deplorable condition. I managed to get out of him that Gemma had left him and she thought we'd been having an affair. He mumbled something about her coming home and finding us together last Sunday and jumping to the wrong conclusion. He said he was going to get blind drunk and left. It was only then that it suddenly hit me what might have happened and I rang you. I suppose he might be home by now at a pinch. You could try there.'

'I'll ring straight away. God, what a mess! You might as well go home, Lenore. There's nothing more you can do here.'

'But I feel so *awful*!' she wailed.

'Just go home,' Celeste bit out, thinking Gemma could only improve with her absence, no matter how innocent she was.

'Wait!' Gemma said and got shakily to her feet. She walked up to Lenore and embraced her. 'I'm sorry I thought all those dreadful things about you,' she cried. 'You've always been sweet to me and I've returned your kindnesses with jealousy and suspicion. I'm so sorry. None of this is your fault. I've been a fool.'

'Oh, Gemma, love,' Lenore said with a sad sigh. 'You've never been a fool. And what happened was not your fault. Any woman would have thought the same thing. And I haven't helped, running to Nathan with my problems all the time. But he loves you, Gemma. For all his faults, he really loves you. Don't throw him away. If you do, you'll destroy him.'

'I don't want to throw him away,' she said with a strangled sob. 'But I don't think he wants me back.'

'Then fight for him,' Lenore urged. 'You love him, don't you?'

'Yes.'

'It's a precious thing, love. It doesn't come your way too often.'

Celeste found her eyes drifting to Byron's but the gaze he returned was so hard that she flinched. He'll never believe how much I love him, she realised wretchedly. He'll never believe how much he's lost...

'I'll go now,' Lenore said, turning to Byron. 'Maybe if you talk to him, Byron. He obviously needs someone to talk to him. To be honest, I'm frightened what he might do.'

He's already done it,' Celeste thought bitterly.

'I will, Lenore,' Byron reassured her. 'Don't worry. Nathan's a reasonable man.'

Celeste only just stopped herself from laughing.

'Here,' Byron said, picking up the script from where it had fallen from Gemma's limp fingers to the floor. 'Take this with you. I think we've seen enough.'

'I don't know how I'm ever going to do that scene now,' Lenore said with a shudder.

'You're an actress, Lenore,' Byron told her with his usual lack of sensitivity. 'Act!'

Celeste returned Gemma to the sofa while Byron shepherded Lenore from Belleview. By the time he returned, Gemma had been persuaded to drink all the brandy and she was sitting there like a zombie.

'I didn't get any answer from Nathan's number,' Byron told them both. 'If he's been drinking he might be out to it. Or maybe he's not at home at all.' He threw Gemma a worried look. 'I think she'd better stay here for the night, Celeste. I'm sure I could find her something to sleep in.'

'She has her luggage with her,' Celeste told him, aware that Gemma seemed incapable of talking. She was almost catatonic, sitting there. 'She was going to go to the airport Hilton tonight and catch a flight back to Lightning Ridge tomorrow.'

'But why? I didn't think she liked it there.'

'She didn't. It was something about unfinished business. Anyway, you go and get the suitcases. They're on the front porch. And then we'll take her upstairs and put her to bed.'

Amazingly, Gemma seemed to go to sleep as soon as her head hit the pillow. Celeste still sat with her for a while, then tucked her in, turned off the bedside lamp and was creeping out when she saw Byron still standing in the doorway, watching her. There was the most peculiar expression on his face which was something akin to pain.

'What?' she whispered. 'What is it?'

He shook his head, abruptly ushering her from the room and closing the door.

'Did you get on to Nathan?' she asked.

'No. He doesn't seem to be home. But I contacted the Hilton and cancelled Gemma's room as well as her flight to Lightning Ridge. She's not going anywhere tomorrow and that's final. She has things to patch up here first.'

'Mmm,' was all Celeste said.

'You don't think she can patch it up with Nathan?'

'We'll see,' she said non-committally.

Byron gave her a narrow-eyed look. 'What do you know that I don't know?'

'Have you got all night?'

'Very funny.'

'I'm tired, Byron,' she said and began striding away from him down the hall. 'I'm going to call a taxi and go home.'

'You don't look tired,' he called after her. 'You look fantastic.'

Celeste ground to a halt, whirling to stare at him standing there, his handsome face unbelievably arrogant as he began blatantly to look her over. Not a second look all night and now this... this blisteringly sexual appraisal.

'You're sex on two legs, Celeste,' he said in a desire-thickened voice, 'and you know it.'

She folded her arms and lifted her chin, but behind her outward cool was a madly beating heart and pounding blood vessels. 'Do you honestly think you can treat me as you treated me when I arrived, then think a couple of tossed-off compliments will get you back in my good books?'

'I'm not interested in being in your good books,' he said with chilling honesty. 'My interests lie elsewhere...'

'No kidding. But if our interests aren't mutual, Byron, then I'm afraid it's a no go.'

'But our interests *are* mutual, Celeste,' he drawled, and started walking slowly towards her. 'Why else would you have come here tonight dressed as you are if you didn't want me to look at you, if you didn't want me to want you, if you didn't want me to do this?'

Celeste was stunned when his hands shot out to drag her into his arms, taking her mouth in a savage kiss while he shoved her back against the wall so hard that all the breath was knocked out of her lungs. He must have crushed his hands in the process but he didn't seem to notice, all his concentration on what he was doing inside her lips.

One of his legs pushed between hers and before she knew what she was doing she had lifted her right leg and

was sliding the inside of her thigh up and down on his.
He groaned into her mouth, and almost immediately his
hands were on the waistband of her jeans and the snap
fastener gave way.

But he didn't proceed any further in that direction.
Instead, his hands crept up under her leather jacket to
mould over her lace-encased breasts, teasing her braless
nipples into rock-hard pebbles till they felt they had to be
bursting through the already tightly stretched material.
He didn't stop kissing at any point and Celeste could feel
her limbs gradually going to jelly. Her leg dropped limply
back to the ground and she would have slid down the wall
to the floor if he hadn't been holding her upright.

'Good lord!' a female voice gasped from somewhere.

Byron wrenched away, Celeste sagging downwards
before propping her back against the wall and levering
herself into a standing position. Her wide, glazed eyes
encountered a strange woman standing there, gaping at
them both. It was a few seconds before she recognised
Ava. Once she did, Celeste's gaze jerked to Byron, who
was raking his hair back from his flushed face in an agitated fashion and trying to calm his ragged breathing.

'You might as well know, Ava,' he said at last.
'Celeste and I have started seeing each other.'

'So I gathered,' his sister returned drily, astonishing
Celeste with her quick composure, not to mention her
appearance. Where had the overweight, awkward, timid
Ava of old gone to? In her place stood an unbelievably
attractive, shapely, confident woman who was looking at
them both with a sardonically arched eyebrow.

'You don't have to answer to me for what you do in
your private life, Byron,' she went on, her voice and face
quite calm now. 'I was merely surprised, that's all. But
it's nice to see that the old feud between the Campbells
and the Whitmores has come to an—er—amicable…
ending. Hello, Celeste.' She nodded politely her way.
'Nice to see you're looking so well. So, Byron, what do
you think of the new carpet?'

'New carpet?'

'You didn't even notice it, did you?' his sister mocked,
and pointed to the long strip of grey-blue carpet that ran

along the middle of the hall. 'It's up the stairs as well. I *did* tell you about it.'

'I'm sure you did. It's—er—very nice.'

'I'm thinking of putting it along the downstairs corridor and through my studio as well. I'm tired of slippery floors.' Ava smothered a yawn, smiling an apology at Celeste. 'Do excuse me. I'm a little weary. I'm going to bed. Will I be expecting an extra for breakfast, Byron?'

Byron, who was not one to be caught at a disadvantage for long, smiled wryly at this unveiled sarcasm from his sister and wickedly said yes.

When Ava looked taken aback,' he added drily, 'Gemma's staying with us for a while. She's asleep in the same room she used to have.'

Ava was frowning now. 'You mean she's left Nathan for good, then?'

'Maybe. Maybe not. We'll talk about the situation in the morning. Go to bed, Ava.'

There was the tone of an order in these last words which Celeste could see Ava resented. Clearly, Byron wasn't ruling the roost around Belleview as he used to.

How times they were a-changing!

Ava shrugged, however, said goodnight and did as she was told. *Not*, Celeste believed, because Byron had ordered her to, but because she wanted to, anyway.

The interruption had given Celeste invaluable time to get herself together and see the situation as Ava had first seen it. Shocking. Disgusting. And deplorable. They'd been acting like two animals, uncaring of anything but their own base needs. Celeste's supposed love for Byron was no excuse for allowing him to use her like that. The least she deserved was a little respect.

Snapping her jeans up again, she surveyed Byron's flushed face with a bitter resentment. It was time this man didn't get his own way for once.

Spinning on the heels of her black boots, she started to march down the hall, quickly reaching the top of the wide marble staircase.

'And where the hell do you think you're going?' Byron called after her.

'Home, Byron. Like I told you.' She kept on going.

'But you can't!'

Her laughter rippled back up the stairwell. 'Just try and stop me.'

'Maybe I could at that,' he snarled, catching up with her as she reached the bottom of the stairs. When she continued across the foyer towards the telephone, he reached out and grabbed her arm.

This time, Celeste had no patience left with him. She grabbed back, flipping him over on to his back on to the marble floor, her boot solidly in the middle of his chest. Though not seriously hurt, he *was* winded. And undeniably shocked.

'Don't presume to touch me again, Byron,' she warned darkly. 'Not unless you're invited. Now I'm going to call a taxi. Stop me at your own peril.'

He didn't try to stop her, and she left five minutes later.

CHAPTER THIRTEEN

'WHAT a pickle!' Ava said over breakfast. 'But surely, Byron, once you explain it all to Nathan, he'll understand why Gemma did what she did.'

'Gemma doesn't seem to think so.'

Ava turned puzzled eyes towards Gemma, who had woken this morning with ambivalent feelings. She wanted very much to do what Lenore had urged her to do—fight tooth and nail to put her marriage right, irrespective of the events of yesterday. But there remained in her heart the feeling that Nathan would never believe she hadn't slept with Damian. He didn't trust her. He didn't trust women in general. His mother had left him with this crippling legacy and Gemma wasn't sure if the love he did hold for her was strong enough to balance the scales in her favour.

'He thinks I went from his bed to Damian Campbell's,' she said with a grim honesty. 'He couldn't conceive that Damian might just want to be my friend.'

'Well, you can't blame him for that, surely,' Byron muttered. 'The man's reputation is hardly lily-white.'

Gemma settled her steeliest gaze upon her father-in-law. 'I don't set much store by people's so-called reputations any more. Till I met Celeste, all I'd heard about her were bad things, but she's not like that at all! She's a warm, wonderful woman and I won't hear a word against her. I won't hear a word against Damian, either. He might not be a saint but he's been very good to me and he's never made a pass or done a single thing to offend me.'

Byron scowled at this while Ava leant over to pat her gently on the wrist. 'It's very creditable of you to defend

your new-found friends, Gemma. I, for one, agree with
you that one can't always believe what is said about
others, but please...understand our concern as well.
There's never been any love lost between the Campbells
and the Whitmores. And you're a Whitmore. Common
sense demands one has to view with suspicion whenever
a Campbell makes friendly overtures towards a
Whitmore, wouldn't you say, Byron?'

Gemma blinked at the savage look Byron sent his sister across the breakfast table. 'We all have to run our own
races in the end, Ava. You, of all people, should appreciate that.'

Ava's returning smile was so self-assured that Gemma
was stunned. The word 'transformation' was not an ex-
aggeration when applied to Ava. She'd fairly blossomed
in every way, not just her looks. There was a confidence
about her person and even her movements that was a
pleasure to see. Gemma had always liked her but had also
always pitied her. No one was ever going to feel pity for
this composed, assertive, attractive woman ever again.

'So what are you going to do, Gemma?' Ava asked.

Byron jumped in before Gemma could verbalise a
plan. 'If she's in agreement, I'd like to drive her over to
see Nathan first thing this morning. Maybe I could have
a word with him first, pave the way, so to speak.
Nathan's likely to still feel highly emotional, and maybe
irrational, about the situation.'

Gemma closed her eyes. God, if Byron did that,
Nathan might tell him what happened yesterday. She
didn't want anyone else to know about it. OK, so
Celeste knew, but she'd sworn her to secrecy. There was
nothing to be gained by blackening Nathan's name to his
family. Clearly he hadn't been himself yesterday. Something had snapped in him and he hadn't been able to see
reason. Gemma could see that now.

'Is that what *you* want, Gemma?' Ava asked kindly,
perhaps interpreting her shut eyes as an unwillingness to
go along with Byron.

She lifted damp lashes to give Ava a small half-smile.
'Yes. The sooner I talk to him, the better. Only...I don't

want you to talk to him first, Byron. Please. I feel this is something private and personal between Nathan and myself. I know you all want to help but I feel we have to work out our problems ourselves. *I* must talk to Nathan, and he must be made to talk to me. *Really* talk, probably for the first time in his life.'

Ava nodded wisely. 'You're quite right. That's always been Nathan's problem. He keeps things to himself too much. He doesn't know how to open up to people.'

'I hate to admit it,' Byron said with a weary sigh, 'but I think you could be right. Even when he was a young lad, he didn't say much. He let me do all the talking. I used to think he was listening, that he was really taking in the advice I was giving him, but how do I know if he ever did? Maybe I failed him. Maybe he wasn't even the essentially good boy I thought he was ... Maybe he's not turned out as well as I'd hoped.'

Gemma suddenly remembered Damian's earlier claim that Nathan had had a sexual liaison with Byron's wife shortly after he came to live with them. How odd, she thought, that now, even after what Nathan had done, her faith in her husband's moral fibre was stronger than ever. Perverse as it might seem, she was sure that there had never been anything between Irene and Nathan. Not ever. Nathan might be capable of a lot of things, but not that kind of treachery.

'Nathan is not easy to understand, Byron,' she told her father-in-law, 'but in his heart he is a good man. You should feel pride in what you've achieved with him. He would surely have been lost if you hadn't taken him in and I know he loves you dearly. He would hate for you ever to think him unworthy as his son, which is another reason why I don't want you to confront him this morning. He might feel belittled somehow in your eyes. That would never do. No, I can't allow that ...'

Byron and Ava were both staring at her as though they couldn't believe what they were hearing. Her smile was softly wry, tears pricking her eyes. 'My love is not blind any more,' she murmured, 'and it's stronger for not being so. Nathan is a man worth fighting for. I won't let misunderstandings come between us, and I won't let his past come between us.'

'He's a lucky man,' Byron muttered. 'It must be really something to have a woman love you like that.'

A hushed silence fell on the table. Ava eventually broke it by abruptly scraping back her chair. 'Anyone for more coffee?'

'I'M GOING TO WAIT outside here,' Byron stated firmly as he slid his Jaguar into the kerb. 'I don't care how long you take. I'll just sit here and read the newspaper till you come back down.'

'I might be ages!' Gemma protested. 'You should go on to your office.'

'And what if things don't work out?'

'But they will,' she insisted, refusing to think of any other outcome.

'I'll wait,' he repeated stubbornly.

'Oh, all right.' She dragged in a steadying breath, letting it out slowly. 'Are you sure Nathan will still be there? I mean...how do you know that after your call this morning he hasn't done a flit? He might not want to see me.'

'He doesn't know it's you who's coming to see him.'

Gemma's head whipped round to stare at him.

'I thought it best,' Byron said ruefully.

Gemma sighed. 'Yes, it probably was.' Still, she was not fond of deception. Suddenly, she was reluctant to make a move to get out, her stomach churning. 'How...how do I look?' she asked nervously.

She'd taken a lot of trouble with her make-up and clothes, choosing a dark green slimline dress which was one of Nathan's favourites. It had a wide self-covered belt that pulled her tiny waist in even further, emphasising her hour-glass figure. A gold chain necklace filled the deep V crossover bodice and gold drop earrings dangled from her ears. Red Door perfume wafted tantalisingly up from where she'd sprayed it between her breasts.

It did cross her mind that it would seem crazy to anyone else that she was making herself physically attractive for the same man who'd virtually raped her the day before. But understanding and love made her see Nathan's actions as an expression of extreme pain, not violence, a reaction to an imagined betrayal that he could not cope with. He had struck out at her in a horrible way, admittedly, and she had been devastated at the time, but there was no future in keeping those feelings of anger and vengeance going. Her future, she felt sure, lay with understanding her husband, and unconditionally loving him.

'I haven't overdone things, have I?'

'You look absolutely delicious,' Byron complimented with such a look Gemma was taken aback for a moment. She'd never thought of her father-in-law as a member of the opposite sex before. He was simply Nathan's adopted father. The formidable head of Whitmore's. An invincible, almost machine-like individual.

Now her woman's eyes took in his strongly handsome face, his penetrating blue eyes, his highly sensual mouth. He might be fifty years old but he didn't look it. In fact, he looked fit enough to go quite a few rounds, either in the ring or in bed.

She almost blushed under her forthright train of thought, but she frowned instead, her mind sliding back to how Celeste had dressed for her meeting with Byron last night. It had struck her as peculiar at the time—Celeste's provocative clothing quite at odds with the occasion. Was the answer sitting behind the wheel in this very car? Who knew? Maybe Byron was the answer to a lot of things Celeste did...

Gemma gave herself a mental shrug. What did Byron and Celeste have to do with what she was about to do?

Nothing!

'I suppose I can't put this off any longer,' she muttered, and opened the passenger door.

'Good luck.'

'Thanks. I think I'm going to need it.'

'Don't forget I'm waiting down here.'

'I won't,' she said and climbed out, striding purposefully over to the building.

Her outward decisiveness was a complete sham, something that struck her forcibly once she found herself in front of the door to their apartment. Should she knock, or let herself in with her own keys? If she knocked and Nathan slammed the door in her face, what could she do then?

Gemma inserted her key with shaking hands,, let herself in then shut the door behind her. Immediately, Nathan appeared outside the door of his study, glaring down the corridor at her. She simply stood there and stared back at him.

Dear God, but he looked appalling. Unshaven. Bloodshot eyes. His hair a mess. Wearing navy blue pyjama bottoms and nothing else.

He didn't say a word as he looked at her. Not a word. But his eyes were dead.

'What are you doing here?' he asked at last in a voice so unlike his she was stunned. There was no anger. No emotion. No nothing.

'Byron brought me. He . . . he's waiting in the car for me downstairs,' Gemma explained shakily. 'Look, I'm sorry he lied to you but he was worried you might not stay if he said it was me who wanted to talk to you.'

'He'd be right. Why in God's name you would want to talk to me at all mystifies me,' he said in that horrible, hollow-sounding voice. 'But it won't make any difference. It's over. We're over.'

When he went to turn away, Gemma blurted out, 'I saw Lenore last night. She explained to me that what I overheard you and Lenore saying to each other last Sunday was actually a section of your play.'

Nathan froze. He didn't turn round, but he waited for her to continue.

'She showed me the actual script,' Gemma went on hurriedly. 'It was exactly what I overheard, word for word. She said it's a scene she'd been having trouble with and you were helping her with it. It's where the leading man tells his leading lady that it was only sex between them the night before. You must know the scene I'm talking about . . .'

'Yes,' he agreed flatly. 'I know the one.'

'Then you must be able to see why I jumped to the wrong conclusion,' she implored. 'That was the only reason I left, I swear to you. And I didn't run straight to Damian. I didn't even contact him till the next day when I couldn't think where to go and what to do. I ... I didn't want to go back to Belleview and I couldn't think of anyone else I knew. Please believe me when I tell you we have not been having an affair, not before I left you or after. I swear to you, Nathan. I'm not lying about this.'

He turned slowly to face her, his eyes totally devoid of expression. 'And you think that would make me feel better? If I allow myself to believe you, my darling Gemma, then I would have no option but to go and blow my brains out. And I'm not going to do that over any woman,' he muttered and disappeared into his study.

Gemma raced after him, arriving in the doorway in time to see him slump down into the armchair in the far corner and lift a half-empty bottle of vodka to his lips. He drank long and hard, eyeing her quite fiercely now over the bottle.

'What happened to all those people you work with?' he challenged when he jerked the bottle away. 'Why couldn't you have gone to one of them?'

She shrugged helplessly. 'I don't know. I didn't think of them.'

'Instead, you thought of Damian Campbell, the last man on earth any husband would want his wife near.'

Gemma fell silent. She was not going to argue with Nathan on this score, but neither was she going to agree with him.

'It's all immaterial anyway,' he muttered darkly, then took another swallow from the bottle. 'As I said before, we're finished. You can have your divorce, and whatever else you want. You'll get no arguments from me.'

'But I don't want a divorce!' she protested wretchedly.

'Don't be so bloody ridiculous,' he scorned. 'No woman would stay married to a man who did what I did yesterday. I dare say you couldn't wait to tell everyone what a disgusting creature you married.'

Gemma flinched, then decided to lie. 'I've told no one, Nathan,' she said huskily. 'No one.'

His eyes narrowed till they were cold slits of steel. 'Byron doesn't know?'

'No.'

He actually shuddered, his obvious distress and self-disgust tearing Gemma's heart out. She rushed forward, dropping to her knees beside his chair, grabbing his free hand. 'Let's forget what happened yesterday, Nathan. You were upset. You didn't know what you were doing. But you do love me. I *know* you love me. I refuse to let one unfortunate incident spoil what we could still have together. I love you and I don't want any other man but you.'

He was staring at her as though she was mad, his eyes wide with disbelief and yes... *revulsion*. He reefed his hand out of hers and pushed her away as he hauled himself to his feet. Lurching across the room, he reached his desk, where he whirled to face her once more. 'What kind of woman are you? How can you dismiss what I did to you so easily? *I* can't. I can't dismiss it any more that I can dismiss in whose bedroom I found you.'

Gemma groaned and shook her head as she got slowly to her feet. 'You're wrong about that, Nathan. So wrong. And you were wrong to do what you did. But love can forgive, can't it?'

'That depends on what it has to forgive.'

Gemma wasn't sure now if he was referring to her forgiving him, or him forgiving her.

'Please, Nathan, let's just forgive each other *everything*! We both did things we regret. It was poor judgement for me to go to Damian for help, but it was also poor judgement for you to have so much to do with Lenore. Can't we just learn from our mistakes and go forward? We love each other. With a little more trust I think we can still have a good marriage.'

'Trust ... Now that's a commodity I think will be in short supply between us from now on, my dear. As for

our loving each other, you never really loved me. Not
your fault, of course. You were very young and I rushed
you into marriage before you could differentiate between lust and love. I'm doing you a favour by letting you
go.'

'And what if I don't *want* to be let go?'

He threw her an impatient scowling look. 'Then I'll
have to *make* you go.' Striding behind the desk, he reefed
opened a drawer and extracted a large brown envelope.
'Remember this?' he asked, waving it at her. 'You asked
me what it was one day and I told you it contained business documents. It doesn't. It's a report from the private
detective I hired to find your mother.'

Gemma could feel the blood drain from her face.
Luckily she was standing next to a chair. Her fingers felt
for the armrest and she leant against it. 'What are you
trying to say, Nathan?' she said in a raw whisper.

'I'm saying I lied to you. He found your mother. *I*
made the decision to keep her identity from you.'

'But . . . but *why*, for pity's sake?' she cried, shattered
by this news. He'd known what finding her mother meant
to her. How could he have done this? This was far worse
than what he did yesterday. Far, far worse!

'What does it matter what my reasons were now? I did
it. Here . . .' He tossed the envelope on to the edge of the
desk. 'Read it. As fate would have it, I doubt the news
will come as a big shock to you as it did to me.'

Gemma stared at the envelope across the room as
though it were a deadly snake. Why would the identity of
her mother come as a shock? Was she a form of low-life?
A prostitute, perhaps? Her father had always said she
was a slut. It was the only explanation for why Nathan
would keep this a secret . . .

'Do excuse me,' Nathan tossed off almost indiffer-
ently. 'Now that I've settled the matter of our divorce,
I'm going to go and clean myself up. I will presume that
once you've read that you'll want to be on your way as
soon as possible.'

Gemma was left feeling sick and alone with his abrupt
departure. Her mind was having difficulty in taking it all

in. She'd wanted to find her mother for so long, and her identity was inside that envelope. All she had to do was look.

Approaching the desk with a madly beating heart, she almost dropped the thing when she first went to pick it up. With it clutched in her hands, she made her way round behind the desk where she slumped gratefully into the chair.

The flap wasn't sealed and it flipped out easily. Gemma drew the dreaded sheets of paper out of their hiding place, her eyes glazed as they skimmed over the printed report, searching for the name.

It jumped out at her as though it were in neon lights, making Gemma catch her breath with shock.

Oh, my God, I don't believe it, came her shaken thoughts. I simply don't believe it! It . . . it's impossible. It doesn't make sense. She can't be my mother. She simply can't be!

CHAPTER FOURTEEN

GEMMA pulled open the passenger door of Byron's Jaguar and climbed in.

'Good God, Gemma!' he exclaimed. 'You're as white as a sheet. What happened? Don't tell me he wouldn't listen to you. And what's that you've got?' he added, staring at the envelope clutched in her hands.

'Nothing. It...it's personal,' she said, still shaken by the contents.

Byron frowned down at the envelope for a moment, then shrugged. 'Well, what about Nathan? Did you talk to him?'

'Nathan?' Gemma's heart hardened against her husband in a way she never thought it would. 'Oh, yes, I talked to him, as much as one ever talks to Nathan. He wants a divorce, and, as far as I'm concerned, he can have it.'

'*What*? But didn't you explain about the mix-up over the play?'

'Yes, but he still doesn't believe me about Damian. Nathan doesn't believe I love him or that I've ever really loved him. Then there are other things as well...'

'What other things?'

'Private things, Byron. Things I can't tell you.'

His sigh was full of frustration. 'Is there any point *my* talking to him?'

'Certainly not today. Maybe not ever. He seemed quite determined to have done with our marriage.' So determined, Gemma realised bitterly, that he had made sure she found out the one thing she *could* not forgive.

All Byron could do was wearily shake his head and start the car. 'Where would you like me to take you? Back to Belleview?'

'No. I...I would appreciate it if you could drop me off outside Campbell's head office.'

Byron's head snapped round, his expression grim. 'I don't care how stubborn or stupid Nathan has been, Gemma, do not go running to Damian Campbell again, I beg of you. Come... let me take you home to Ava. A nice long chat with a sympathetic lady is what you need.'

'I don't want to go to Campbell's to see Damian,' she said shakily. 'I need to see Celeste.'

'*Celeste*?'

'Yes.' Gemma had no intention of offering Byron an explanation at this traumatic juncture and he had enough intelligence to quickly size up her fragile yet determined mood.

'All right. But promise you'll take a taxi home to Belleview when you're finished there.'

'I promise.'

It was only a short drive from Elizabeth Bay into the city and within no time Gemma was presenting herself at Reception at Campbell's, where she stood waiting while the receptionist took a couple of incoming calls. This didn't help her underlying agitation, or her growing sense of awe at the amazing set of circumstances that had led to this moment.

'May I help you?' the receptionist asked politely once she finished answering the telephone.

'I need to see Miss Campbell. I don't have an appointment but if you tell her it's Gemma Whitmore and it's very important, I'm sure she'll see me.'

The receptionist spoke briefly to someone on the telephone after which she looked up and flashed Gemma a bright smile. 'Miss Campbell will see you immediately. It's the last door down that corridor. Go straight on in and her secretary will take you to her.'

CELESTE WAS besieged with uncharacteristic butterflies from the moment her secretary came through with the message from Gemma. She waited impatiently for her to be shown in, wondering what could be so urgent. The sudden thought that Gemma might have gone to see Nathan and been assaulted again brought with it a sickening surge which sent her leaping to her feet the moment the door opened. Worried eyes searched the girl's face as she walked in and closed the door behind her. While she did not look overly distraught, an underlying agitation was evident in her pale face and slightly hesitant movements.

'What is it?' Celeste asked, thoroughly agitated herself now. 'What's happened?'

When Gemma couldn't seem to find her voice, simply standing there with unexpected tears filling her eyes, Celeste almost panicked. Her first instinct was to race around the desk and go to her, but something in Gemma's face kept her rooted to the spot.

'What *is* it?' she asked again, a nervously fluttering hand coming up to her throat. She watched, her nerves stretching, as the girl visibly battled for composure.

'I . . . I'm not sure how you're going to take this news,' Gemma said haltingly.

'What news?'

'Oh, God . . . I can't . . . I just can't. You . . . you'd better read this.' And she came forward to place a large brown envelope on her desk. 'You'd better sit down.'

Celeste blinked. Sit down? Good God, what was in this envelope?

But she did as she was told, sat down and drew out several pages of what looked like a typed report. From the moment she saw the faded photograph attached, her stomach clenched down hard.

Celeste read each page with a fearful, yet excited anticipation welling up within her. This couldn't be true, she kept saying to herself. And yet is was. It *was*!

Her eyes flew up, locking with Gemma's suddenly tearful ones.

'You *are* my mother, aren't you?' the girl said, hopefully, pleadingly.

Celeste choked up totally, her head swimming as the force of emotion hit. All she could manage was a weak nod.

Then Gemma smiled and Celeste's heart burst open, all the pain of the past years obliterated by that one beautifully loving gesture.

'Mother,' Gemma said softly, and held out her arms.

With a strangled sob Celeste ran to her daughter, falling into her arms in an embrace that held all the unused love in her heart. 'Oh, my darling child,' she wept. 'My daughter. Oh, God, I don't believe it...'

'Believe it, Mother. Believe it.'

Celeste pulled back, stunned by the composure of this lovely girl who was her own beautiful little baby grown up. Her shaking hand reached out to trace over her hair and face. 'I...thought you were lost to me forever,' she said shakily. 'You were stolen from me, you know, like the detective suggested might have happened in that report. I didn't give you away, I promise you. And I did try to find you. Not with any success, unfortunately. I thought...I...I...'

The tears took over again and she could not go on.

Gemma pulled her back into a bear-hug. 'I knew that if you were alive somewhere,' she said firmly, 'one day, *I* would find *you*.'

Mother and daughter hugged for a while till Celeste drew back with a still bewildered look on her face. 'I still can't believe it. You don't understand what this means to me. You could never understand.'

You are my only child, came the wrenchingly emotional thought. The only child I will ever have.

But it didn't seem the right moment to say that.

'You're so beautiful,' she said, once again tracing trembling fingers over her daughter's sweet face.

Gemma smiled that heart-stoppingly sweet smile of hers, making Celeste go to mush once more.

'I must take after my mother,' she said generously.

Celeste's groan was tortured. 'Are you sure you want someone like me as your mother?'

'I'm proud to have you as my mother,' Gemma insisted warmly.

'But... but what about my reputation?'

'Are you talking about the lovers you've had? Why should you be judged so harshly for that? You're not married and you're still a very beautiful woman. You have every right to be loved.'

'But... but...'

'Do you think I'm shocked because you've had relationships with younger men? Why should I be? Nathan is many years older than I am. Age has nothing to do with love.'

'Would you believe me if I told you none of those young men was my lover?'

There was no doubting Gemma was startled. But she quickly gathered herself to speak in a reassuringly firm voice. 'Of *course* I would believe you! Why would you lie? But my love isn't conditional on such things. You're my mother! I love you as I've always loved you, even without knowing you. And now that I know you didn't deliberately leave me with my father, I don't even feel angry with you any more.'

Celeste was jolted by this. She hadn't yet thought of what Gemma's life had been like with that ghastly man. Oh, the poor darling, the poor, poor darling...

Her expression was anguished as she reached out to her daughter again, though it was so good to just touch her, to gaze into her lovely eyes while she stroked her lovely hair. 'He didn't... mistreat you, did he? I don't think I could bear that...'

'He tried to be a good father,' Gemma said. 'I think he loved me, but he was a hard man to live with.'

'How... how did he die?'

'Fell down a mine shaft. Or was pushed. I... I've always felt guilty that I wasn't able to grieve for him as a daughter should. To be honest, he and I never saw eye to eye. Ma says we weren't at all alike.'

Celeste's heart contracted. Should she tell her the truth? Was there anything to be gained by giving her more shocks? Not only that, did she dare bring in another party, who might try to take from her what she had only just found?

'Who's Ma?' she asked, stalling for time as she pondered this dilemma.

'An old lady neighbour of mine at Lightning Ridge. Everyone calls her Ma. She was very kind to me.'

'Lightning Ridge again,' Celeste muttered to herself. 'And this Ma thought you had none of your father in you?'

'Not a scrap.'

Celeste made up her mind. She couldn't let this lovely girl go through life thinking that bastard was her father. Maybe if Gemma had loved Stefan then she would not have said a word. But she deserved better than that.

'That's because he wasn't your father,' she said tautly, and held her breath.

Did those big brown eyes light up with shock, or relief?

'Then who?' Gemma asked. 'W...who was my father?'

Celeste gulped in a deep breath, aware that her heart was racing madly. Much as she felt Byron had been greatly at fault in their own relationship, he was a father to be proud of. Lifting her chin, she spoke with a quiet dignity. 'Byron Whitmore.'

Gemma took a staggering step backwards. 'B-Byron? Byron is my *father*?'

Celeste nodded. 'Perhaps you should sit down this time, darling,' she suggested softly, 'and I'll tell you all about it.' She guided the stunned child over to the chesterfield and settled her down. 'Perhaps a little drink would be in order as well? Coffee perhaps, or something stronger?'

Gemma grabbed her hands to stop her from walking away, drawing her down beside her. 'No, nothing. I'm all right. It...it just took my breath away for a moment.'

Celeste's smile was gently wry. 'Your father has always done the same to me. Taken my breath away...'

'You...you loved him, then?'

'I've never loved any other man.'

'And does he know about me?'

She shook her head. 'No. He doesn't even know we had a child together.'

'You have to tell him, Celeste,' she urged.

'Let me tell you first. I want you to know it all, so that you can understand . . .'

Celeste hesitated, knowing that she didn't have to tell Gemma the basic background details of the man she'd believed was her father all these years. It was well documented in the report that his real name was Stefan Bergman, and he'd come to Australia from Sweden in the Sixties to go prospecting in the opal fields of Coober Pedy in South Australia. When he'd struck it rich there, he'd come to Sydney to sell his finds and live it up big. It was also in the report that he'd started dating the pretty daughter of Stewart Campbell and several weeks later they'd both caught a plane for Europe, choosing to stay in Spain once it became obvious she was having a baby.

What the report didn't include was why Celeste had chosen to go with him in the first place.

God, but it was hard to tell her own daughter that she'd committed adultery with her own half-sister's husband and become pregnant by him, and that she'd run off with Stefan on the rebound. It sounded so appalling in the telling. Yet there was nothing but sympathy for her in her daughter's soft brown eyes when she at last found the courage to look at her.

'You really loved Byron, didn't you?' Gemma murmured.

Celeste nodded. 'Madly. We'd been lovers briefly when I was only seventeen. I thought he was in love with me too but he broke it off, saying it was only a sexual thing. I was devastated when he married Irene a few months later.'

'I've heard some terrible things about her,' Gemma said frowning. 'Why did Byron marry her? Surely he couldn't have been in love with her?'

'I don't think he was, but she was very beautiful and madly in love with him. People always said he married her to get his hands on Campbell Jewels but my father left total control of the company in my mother's hands. Whatever, the marriage was not a happy one. To be honest, I think Byron might have married me if Irene hadn't told him some rather damning lies about me. She made Byron believe I was a little tramp who slept with anything in trousers. Which wasn't true, I assure you. Byron had been my only lover at that stage.'

Gemma was shaking her head. 'Why was she so mean?'

Celeste shrugged. 'I don't really know. She always resented my mother, even though her own mother died soon after she was born. My mother tried to be nice to her but truly I can't remember a time when Irene wasn't very difficult to live with.'

'Byron should have divorced her and married you,' Gemma said. 'He must have loved you. He wouldn't have made love to you while he was married if he didn't.'

Celeste's heart leapt before she got it back under control. Gemma was only twenty, and twenty-year-olds could be very idealistic. 'I don't know about that, Gemma. Men can fall prey to lust more easily than women. I was very wrong to kiss him that day. I wanted to see if I was over him. Clearly, I wasn't,' she finished drily.

'So what happened?' Gemma asked.

'Irene caught us together soon afterwards and guessed what had happened. She didn't say a word, simply looked at both of us then walked out of the room. Byron turned on me and called me all sorts of names.'

'Which is why you went off with my father.'

'You mean Stefan.'

'Oh . . . yes . . . I keep forgetting.'

Celeste fell silent, not wanting to tell Gemma about her eventual disillusionment over the man she'd thought such a gentleman. She especially did not want to see the horror in those innocent brown eyes if the whole truth was revealed.

Even so, Gemma was frowning. 'I presume he thought I was his,' she said.

'Yes,' came Celeste's reluctant admission.

'And you refused to marry him, I suppose. Is that why he stole me?'

'Something like that.'

'Yet you stayed with him till I was born. Why did you do that?'

'I...I wasn't in the best of health and he...he said he wanted to take care of me.'

Gemma's frown deepened. 'Doesn't sound like the man I knew. Still...I suppose he might have been a kind person once. Maybe he changed once he realised you didn't love him. Maybe he became bitter and twisted.'

'Yes, I think that's what must have happened,' Celeste was happy to let her daughter believe this. Better than the ghastly truth.

'But what about the opal? You know...the Heart of Fire.'

Celeste's heart missed a beat. 'The...the Heart of Fire?'

'Yes. I found it along with that photograph after Dad died. I...I mean...after the man I *thought* was my father died.'

'Good God,' Celeste murmured. 'I didn't realise... So Byron was telling the truth all along. It *was* found in a dead miner's belongings out at Lightning Ridge.'

'It certainly was. I thought I was rich for a while till I found out it was stolen. What I'd like to know is...if...if Mr Bergman was rich back then, why did he steal it...and *how*?'

Celeste flushed. 'He didn't steal it initially. Though he did later. From me. I was the original thief.'

'*You*!'

'Byron was going to give it to Irene on their wedding-day to symbolise the healing of the rift between our two families. I...I took it that day, vowing never to let the rift heal between the Whitmores and the Campbells.

'Oh...'

'It was very wrong of me.'

'Understandable, though.'

'Do you really understand, Gemma?' Celeste said pleadingly.

Gemma clasped her mother's hands tightly in hers. 'Of course. Loving someone as much as you love my father can make one do insane things.'

'Yes.' Celeste muttered bleakly. 'Yes, it can . . .'

'You still love him, don't you?'

Celeste blinked her amazement at this intuitive guess.

'I suspected as much when I saw you together last night,' Gemma explained gently.

'He . . . he's all I've ever wanted,' Celeste confessed brokenly.

'Then go to him. Tell him everything you've just told me. Tell him the truth.'

The truth . . .

Dear God, this sweet child didn't know the half of it.

'Please, Mother,' Gemma begged. 'For me . . .'

Celeste melted. 'All right, my darling. For you . . .'

CHAPTER FIFTEEN

CELESTE was a nervous wreck by the time she knocked on the hotel suite door. Byron wrenched it open immediately, a smouldering scowl on his handsome face.

'You do pick your moments, Celeste,' he grumbled. 'What could be so urgent that you had to see me immediately? And why, if it's not my body you want, did you choose to meet me here of all places?'

A wry smile tugged at her lips. Same old Byron, always huffing and puffing when he was caught at a disadvantage. Well, he *was* at a disadvantage, there was no doubt about that. He was also about to get the shock of his life, if she was any judge. Would it be a welcome shock? Or would the thought of a woman like herself's having had his child turn his stomach?

She'd never had the courage to tell him, first because of his marriage to Irene and secondly because she'd been afraid of his reaction. She could not have borne to see the scorn and scepticism on his face. Even if she'd been able to find their baby—and my God, she had tried—there had been no DNA tests to prove paternity all those years ago. Byron would have scoffed at her claim that he was the father. He would have seen this as another evil attempt of hers to break up his marriage.

But now, his daughter was living in his own home. The truth was an easy matter to prove in the Nineties. Three simple blood-tests and Byron would not be able to deny his paternity.

Celeste hoped and prayed he wouldn't want to. Not for her sake, but for Gemma's. Celeste's heart turned over as she thought of her daughter. How lovely she was, and how loving. Gemma deserved everything good in life,

which included a father who would open his heart to her
and give her all the love and support she needed at this
difficult time in her life. She was having a tough enough
time as it was with that rotten husband of hers.

Fancy Nathan's deliberately keeping her mother's
identity from her when he must have known what it
meant to her! Then, on top of that and everything else
he'd done, he still had the hide to insist on a divorce because of her supposed affair with Damian. The man was
a raving nutcase! Truly, Gemma was better out of the
marriage, a decision she'd thankfully come to herself.
Celeste would never feel happy with her daughter staying married to anyone as unstable and abusive as
Nathan had already proven to be.

But that didn't mean the girl was happy about the situation. She loved that man so much it was quite depress-
ing. Love like that could be incredibly self-destructive...

'For pity's sake, Celeste,' Byron muttered impatiently. 'Are you going to stay standing in the doorway all
afternoon, or are you going to come inside and tell me
what this is all about?'

Celeste stared at him. Why do I love you so much,
Byron? she asked herself for the umpteenth time. What
have you ever done to deserve such undying devotion?

Shaking her head more at herself than him, she
brushed past him, moving along the corridor and into the
sitting area of the suite. Placing her bag on the large low
table between the two sofas, she walked over to briefly
admire the harbour view from the window before turning her back on it to face a frustrated-looking Byron.

'How about pouring me a whisky?' she said. 'And get
yourself one, while you're at it.'

He threw her a disgruntled glare before shrugging and
walking over to open the cabinet that housed the mini-
bar. 'I take it this is going to be bad news,' he said curtly.
'No doubt something to do with Gemma.'

Celeste caught her breath. 'Why do you say that?'

'A logical deduction. I was the one who dropped her
off outside Campbell's after her unsuccessful reconcili-
ation with Nathan this morning. I concluded she must

have found in you a sympathetic woman's ear, something that has been very lacking in her life so far.' He turned and brought the two glasses over, handing her one and lifting his own to his mouth. 'So what's the problem?' he asked after a couple of sips. 'Does she want to live with you at Campbell Court instead of at Belleview?'

'We haven't discussed that yet,' Celeste hedged.

'But it's on the agenda?'

'Maybe...'

'I would never feel comfortable with her living under the same roof as Damian, Celeste,' he pronounced pompously. 'I'll advise her against it, most strongly. She'd be safer at Belleview with me and Ava.'

'I'm sure Damian will not be any danger to Gemma... once I tell him what I'm about to tell you.' Damian was going to be rocked to his socks when he found out he was Gemma's uncle! But no more than Byron was going to be.

Celeste swallowed. How did one say news like this? Really, there was no other way but to just say it but dear God, her tongue suddenly felt thick in her mouth and a trembling had started up deep inside.

'For pity's sake, Celeste, would you just spit it out?' Byron growled.

His impatience was just the impetus she needed.

'Gemma is my daughter,' she blurted out.

Celeste knew that for the rest of her life she would never again see such an expression on Byron's face. Stunned did not describe it. Clearly, he was so shocked and astonished that he was rendered speechless.

Or was his goldfish-mouth stare an expression of disbelief?

'It's true,' she insisted, and walked over to snap open her carry-all and draw out the brown envelope. 'Gemma left this with me so that I could show it to you. It's a report from a private investigator. There's a photo too which she found in her father's things after his death. She told me that's what prompted her desire to search for me in the first place and was the main reason she came to

Sydney. Anyway, Nathan hired a detective agency on Gemma's behalf some time ago but the bastard told her they hadn't been able to find her mother. Only this morning did he produce this, possibly because he considered such an unforgivable deception would make Gemma agree to a divorce.'

Byron took the envelope, still in an obvious state of shock.

'Sit down and read it,' Celeste suggested, her voice sounding firm despite her insides being an utter mess. What would Byron do when he was told the rest? He already looked pole-axed.

Slumping down on to one of the sofas, he put his whisky down and shakily extracted the report from the envelope. Celeste filled the intervening minutes while he read the report by drinking her whisky, refilling her glass and drinking that as well. Slowly, the alcohol seeped into her system, bringing with it a false sense of calm.

Finally, Byron dropped the report into his lap, but kept staring down at the photograph for ages, running his fingers over it. Finally, he looked up at her, his face ashen.

'Gemma never showed me this,' he said in an uncharacteristically subdued voice. 'Maybe I would have recognised you. But probably not, with those sunglasses on. And your face is so thin and drawn. Not as I remembered you...' He frowned down at the photograph again. 'I take it the baby you're carrying here was Gemma?'

'Yes,' she choked out.

'So you were able to have children back then, it seems,' he muttered, an angry colour seeping back into his face. 'Whatever happened to make you barren must have happened after this.' His eyes snapped up, hard and glittering and accusing. 'One doesn't have to be a genius to guess what you did. This hospital stay when you got back to Australia explains all. Clearly, babies did not fit into Celeste Campbell's lifestyle. One mistake was enough, so you made sure there wouldn't be another.'

'That's not true!' Celeste gasped. 'I would never do a thing like that.'

'No? From what I've heard and seen for myself, there isn't anything you wouldn't do, Celeste, to ensure your sex life fulfils all your very demanding expectations. An unwanted pregnancy would curtail your activities for far too long. So tell me about this man,' he went on savagely, jabbing at the photo with a furious finger. 'This Stefan you *gave* your child to. I don't believe that other rubbish. Where did you meet him? Why did you go to Europe with him? Why have a baby by him? Was it that he was simply so good in bed you got carried away one night and forgot to take precautions?'

Celeste stared at Byron, disbelief changing to dismay and despair. She should have known Byron would always believe the worst of her. It was par for the course. This time, however, something snapped inside Celeste and she couldn't even find a righteous anger to fight back with. Her normally rebellious spirit began draining from her and she swayed slightly on her feet. Fearful of actually collapsing, she turned and walked slowly towards the window, where she stood for a moment before turning to glance back over at a still scowling Byron.

'I did not give Stefan my baby,' she said in an empty voice. 'He stole her.'

'Bulldust!' Byron scoffed. 'No one could take anything from you, Celeste, unless you wanted them to.'

Celeste was too tired to stop the ghastly memories from rushing back, or in stopping the emotional devastation they always caused. 'I woke one day to find him packed and the baby's cradle already empty. He told me not to bother trying to find either him or the child because I never would.'

'And you didn't try to stop him?'

'Oh, yes . . . I tried.'

'And what happened?'

'He beat me to a pulp and left me there alone to die.'

There was no satisfaction in Byron's shocked gasp. Or any confidence that he now believed her. Neither did she really care any more.

'My mother can vouch for what I'm saying,' she continued in a dead, flat voice. 'She spoke to the Spanish doctors who treated me, and paid for the hospital bill in Barcelona.' Celeste felt the tears welling up and she turned her face away, clutching at the curtains for support. 'I was taken into emergency surgery where, among other things, I was given a hysterectomy. I nearly died,' she admitted hoarsely. 'Occasionally, over the past twenty years, I wished I had ...'

Celeste's head and shoulders drooped in defeat. For even if Byron believed her now, it wouldn't be enough. Underneath, she had been wanting more than his belief. She had been wanting his understanding and sympathy.

The unexpected feel of Byron's arms closing over her shoulders in what seemed to be a gentle, comforting gesture broke what little was left of her control.

'Oh, God,' she sobbed, and, whirling, threw herself into his arms. 'I'm telling the truth,' she cried against the broad expanse of his chest, tears streaming down her face. 'I swear to you ... I'm telling the truth!'

'Hush,' he soothed, his warm strong arms holding her tightly but tenderly. 'I know you are. No one would make up a horror story like that, least of all you, Celeste. Least of all you ...'

'I tried to find her,' she wept brokenly. 'I spent a fortune on private investigators, but he was far too clever ... and in the end I had to stop or go mad!'

'There, there, don't distress yourself any further. You've found her again, haven't you? And if I know Gemma, she will have no feelings for you but love. She's a daughter to be so proud of, Celeste. One in a million.'

Celeste drew back, dashing away her tears and looking almost imploringly into his eyes. 'I...I'm so glad you think that, Byron. I was hoping you would, because you see ... you see ...'

'What?' he asked, an instant wariness zooming into his eyes. But as Celeste struggled to make that final shocking confession, the penny dropped and his eyes flared with shock. 'No,' he rasped. 'No ...'

'Yes!' she cried. 'It's true. Gemma's *your* daughter, Byron. Not Stefan's. She's yours!'

For a few seconds, his face far surpassed the way it had
looked before, till a dark fury filled his cheeks and a wild
glittering began blazing away in his bright blue eyes. '*My*
daughter? Gemma's *my* daughter?'

Oh, God, Celeste agonised. He's not going to believe
me. 'Yes!' she insisted fiercely. 'I was no longer on the
Pill when we made love that last time. I didn't need to be.
There'd been no one else but you.'

He pushed her away, marching across the room before spinning round and glaring at her. 'And you didn't
tell me? You let that mongrel bastard steal my daughter
and you didn't tell me?'

This totally unjustified slap in the face revived some of
Celeste's old fighting spirit. 'Don't you take that tone
with me, Byron Whitmore. You know damned well you
wouldn't have believed me if I'd come to you and said I
was expecting your baby. Not that I didn't think of doing it. My God, I probably still would have if I hadn't by
then been overseas in the hands of a man so vicious and
vile and cruel that I lived every day in fear of my life.'

'Then why go with him in the first place?'

'Because he wasn't like that at first, you stupid man!
He seemed sweet and kind and gentlemanly, the complete opposite to the man I was in love with but who
wanted nothing to do with me!'

Byron groaned.

'He *said* he loved me,' Celeste swept on. 'Said I was his
ideal woman. He asked me to marry him and on the rebound from my last encounter with you I agreed. We
were on our way to Sweden to visit his family when he
found out I wasn't a virgin. I'd just realised I was pregnant with your child, you see, and in a panic I decided if
I went to bed with Stefan he wouldn't know it wasn't *his*
child. It was a stupid thing to do but I did it anyway. You
do stupid things when you're nineteen and mixed-up and
dreadfully unhappy.

'Anyway, Stefan went off his brain when he realised he
wasn't the first. He beat me so badly that I had to stay in
bed in the hotel room for two weeks. He didn't even call
a doctor. I've never been so terrified in my life. Or so in-

timidated. God, I know now why battered wives don't leave their abusive husbands. You become too frightened. And you lose all your confidence. After that, Stefan decided I wasn't fit to be his wife, but by then he'd become sexually obsessed with me. Every night, I would have to submit to him or be beaten. I was so terrified I let him do whatever he liked, but even then sometimes he still hit me. It was as if I had to be punished for his wanting me all the time. Finally, when I could safely convince him it was his child I was carrying, I told him I was pregnant.'

'Did he believe you?'

She nodded. 'The beatings stopped then, although the threat was always there. He took me to this remote mountain village in Spain to have the baby, and a week after she was born he stole her from me.'

'My God, if the bastard wasn't already dead,' Byron ground out, 'I'd go and kill him with my bare hands.'

Celeste's tormented eyes flew to Byron. 'You... you believe me now?' she choked out. 'You're not angry with me any more? You understand what happened?'

His shoulders sagged, his face full of anguish and remorse. 'Do you think so poorly of me, Celeste, that you imagine I have no feelings? No heart? No conscience? Of course I understand. Only too well. I drove you into the arms of a monster, but *I'm* the one who's the monster for turning my back on the only woman I ever really loved. I didn't have the courage to live what I see now could have been a beautiful dream, simply because I feared it was my worst nightmare.'

Celeste heard nothing except that she was the only woman he'd ever loved. Her heart swelled to bursting point and with it the tears flowed anew. Byron strode back to gather her in and if she hadn't known better she might have thought he cried too for a short while.

'I did fall in love with you,' he admitted huskily. 'So wildly and so passionately that it worried me sick. I always thought that kind of love was like a disease, an unhealthy thing that made men do wicked and reckless things which had the potential to destroy their own and other people's lives. I was a ready and willing victim for Irene's lies about you—oh, yes, I can see now that they were lies—and I sought refuge from my feelings by escaping into a marriage which could never make me feel the same earth-shattering madness I felt when I was with you. I know people said I married Irene for Campbell Jewels, but that's not true. I married her because I thought it would make me safe from the type of love my father had felt for my mother, the consequences of which have haunted me all my life.'

Surprise had Celeste pulling out of Byron's arms. 'But people always talked about your mother and father as being the perfect couple. What was wrong with their love for each other?'

'Didn't your father ever tell you, Celeste? You must have wondered what happened between Stewart Campbell and David Whitmore to start off such a vicious feud in the first place. After all, they'd been best mates ever since they met on the boat that brought them to Australia as emigrants from the UK. They did everything together. When times got tough and jobs were hard to come by, they went mining together. Didn't you ever wonder what could have happened to destroy such a strong bond? It wasn't some silly argument over that opal, I can assure you.'

'Of course I did. But Dad never talked about the old days. He always clammed up whenever I asked him. All I know is he was still best friends with your father when the war broke out because they joined up together.'

'They were best friends up till the time my father was wounded in 1943 and was sent home early.'

'But how would that have ruined their friendship?'

'Your father sent my father to his own home to recuperate. To his wife.'

'His *wife*?' Celeste was confused. 'But Dad didn't marry Irene's mother till after the war.'

'He was married to *my* mother first,' Byron said drily.

Celeste gasped her shock. 'You don't mean ...'

'Yes, that's exactly what I mean. Can you imagine what your father felt when he came home on leave to find his beloved Lucy with *me* growing in her belly?'

'Oh, God, Byron. Knowing his pride and his ego, he would have been devastated. And so hurt! No wonder he hated your father with such a passion.'

'And no wonder he kept the real reason a secret. My own father did the same, but when I was about twelve your father came round to see my father. They had the most awful row. It started about their business rivalry but soon all the old ugliness came out. I couldn't help but overhear every word and it made a big impression on me at the time. I was utterly appalled at my father, who'd always been so strong on morals, yet he himself was nothing but the worst kind of adulterer. All he could say to excuse himself was that he couldn't help himself. He'd fallen madly in love and that was it. He made it sound as though everything was totally out of his control. And he did something that shocked me even more. He started to cry, blubbering away that he was sorry. He begged your father to accept the Heart of Fire as a symbol of his sorrow and remorse—apparently he'd found it while your father was still at the front and this was the second time he'd offered it—but your father spat on him and stormed out.

'I decided that very day that that kind of love had to be the worst thing in the world. I vowed never to succumb to such a destructive disease. Never would a woman be able to make me do anything against my better judgement. Never! And I managed very well, till I was twenty-seven years old. Then, one day, this vision of loveliness walked into my office and I was a goner...' His expression was apologetic and rueful at the same time. 'So you see, Celeste, there are excuses for what we both did, don't you think? Can we perhaps forgive each other and start again? Or is it too late for that?'

'It's never too late to love one another, Byron.'

His relieved but joyous smile was rather wonderful, she thought. Suddenly, she glimpsed the real man behind the arrogant and sometimes impossible façade. Byron had more strength and passion in his little finger than most men had in their whole bodies.

As if to confirm this unspoken realisation, he swept her into his arms and kissed her with a hunger that was as catching as it was comforting.

'You know, Celeste...' he murmured some time later. They were curled up on the sofa together, Celeste half on Byron's lap, her head on his chest, her arms around his waist. 'I knew last night you weren't the woman you'd projected all these years. I saw you with Gemma, being so kind and caring, and I said to myself...that's no hard-hearted, sex-mad bitch there. There's a good woman, a woman worth loving. Naturally, I panicked anew and set out to prove once again that there was nothing to my feelings but lust. Till you put me in my proper place,' he added with a dry chuckle.

'Oh, and where's that?'

'Under your heel?'

'I thought you once said it was in your bed.'

'And so it is. But only if that's where you want to be too.'

They looked at each other and Celeste felt an intense surge of desire. Maybe Byron was right. Maybe their love was a bit of a sickness. But if it was, it was a terminal one, for both of them. It had survived all these years and remained as powerful as ever to this very day. The thrill of being in his arms was as strong as it had been the first time. 'I want to be there every night of my life,' she whispered.

His head dropped to kiss her very, very slowly. 'You do realise my family is going to be scandalised if I marry you,' he said softly against her tingling lips.

'*My* family is going to be scandalised if I marry *you*.'

'Looks as if there are going to be a lot of scandalised people around Sydney, then, aren't there? Because I am going to marry you, Celeste Campbell. I'm going to do what I should have done over twenty years ago. Make an honest woman out of you.'

'Don't ask for miracles, Byron,' she teased. 'Marriage won't necessarily make an honest woman out of me.'

His head jerked back, his face stern. 'If you look at another young man again,' he warned, 'there's going to be hell to pay.'

'There's nothing wrong with looking, Byron. After all, that's all I've ever done.'

His face was both disbelieving and shocked. 'Are you saying...?'

'It was all pretence. I never slept with any of them.'

'Not even that hunk of a chauffeur you batted your eyelashes at and flirted with like mad?'

'Why do you think I had to let him go? I pretended so well he thought he was on to a sure thing.'

'What about that smarmy-looking Luke in the office?'

'Luke is a very clever, ambitious young man who only has designs on Campbell Jewels, not the boss.'

'God, I'm glad to hear that.'

'Say you love me again,' she rasped as she drew him down on to the sofa with her.

'I love you,' he moaned. 'More than I can say.'

'Then don't say it, darling. Show me. Show me how much.'

'I LOVE YOU,' she told him afterwards for the umpteenth time, clasping her to him and refusing to let their bodies separate. 'I've always loved you.'

Byron gave a small groan. 'Don't make me feel guilty any more, Celeste. I can't bear it. When I think of what I put you through. I don't deserve your sweet forgiveness.'

'I put you through a few things myself,' she murmured, and snuggled into him. 'Have you guessed yet that it was me who stole the Heart of Fire?'

'Good God!' Byron rolled her on top of him so he could look up into her eyes. 'You little devil! But how did that Stefan creep get hold of it?' he frowned. 'You didn't give it to him, did you?'

'Never in a million years. He found it in my things and stole it as he stole my little girl. Maybe that's why he never sold it in the end, because he was afraid I would be able to trace the sale to him. Gemma told me all about finding it in his things and bringing it to you. Wasn't that an incredible coincidence? But you've no idea how upset I was when it turned up again. I was torn between setting out on another potentially fruitless search for my baby and trying to put it out of my mind. Of course I couldn't, not when the opal's presence in Australia meant my baby might be here somewhere as well. I went to that ball, determined to find out the circumstances of its return, but found myself buying the damned thing instead, then eventually launching myself into a mad affair with the one man I had vowed never to let touch me again!'

'*You* ought to talk. I've been going to the dogs ever since the night you turned up at that damned ball! I haven't been able to think straight for wanting to be with you. I did all sorts of stupid things to try to put you out of my mind!'

Celeste laughed. 'We're a right pair, aren't we?'

'Yes,' Byron said with sudden seriousness. 'We are a right pair. Right for each other. Right in every way. Maybe it's taken me over twenty years to realise it but now that I have I'm never going to let you go, my darling. You're going to be mine, 'for better for worse, for richer for poorer, in sickness and in health . . . till death us do part'.'

Celeste's eyes swam, her heart swelling with love. 'Ditto, my sweet,' she choked out. 'Ditto.'

CHAPTER SIXTEEN

'YOU'RE right about the sequence of events being quite incredible,' Byron remarked on their way to Belleview later that afternoon. 'Really, if it hadn't been for your stealing the Heart of Fire from me in the first place, that opal would never have got into Bergman's hands, which means it wouldn't have come into Gemma's possession at his death. Without it, she might never have come to us in Sydney at all. She would not have married Nathan and subsequently put the search for you into action. As I said ... amazing!'

Celeste darted him a wary look. 'So, am I forgiven for being the original thief?'

'Of course. In your position, I probably would have done the same thing. God, Celeste, it should have been you I married that day. My marriage to Irene was a disaster from day one.'

'I often wondered how you stood it,' Celeste said truthfully. 'Though I could see Irene was a different person with you than she was with anyone else.'

'I put my head in the sand a lot where she was concerned. It was easier than admitting what a horrendous mistake I'd made. That's always been a great failing of mine, Celeste, not admitting my mistakes or going back on what I've always believed. But not any more, I hope. That boating accident where Irene was killed and I was badly hurt gave me a lot of time to re-evaluate my life and my beliefs. Then, something else happened to bring a different perspective into my life, and a lot of other people's lives around Belleview, I think.'

'What was that, Byron?'

He sent such a warm loving look her way, Celeste melted. 'A lovely young woman came to live with us,' he said softly, 'bringing with her so much simple joy and caring that we all began to wake up to ourselves. The more I think about it, the more I realise how much like you Gemma is, when you were her age. There is a strength and vitality about her that is so endearing. And a sensuality that can be very disturbing. It's almost a relief to find out she's my daughter. Now I can stop having wicked thoughts about her.'

'Byron!'

He laughed. 'Only teasing, darling. But it is a relief to know that that sinful brother of yours has been relegated to the role of her uncle.'

'Yes, I thought of that myself. But I think he'll be thrilled. I'm sure he genuinely likes Gemma as a person, not just as a female.'

'Well, I'll have to take your word for that,' came his dry comment. 'You wouldn't be able to talk him into going and seeing Nathan, would you? If he could convince him that there was nothing between him and Gemma, then everything would be perfect. Gemma and Nathan would get back together again.'

Celeste stiffened. 'I'm not sure that would be so perfect for Gemma. If Nathan didn't believe her when she swore she'd been faithful, do you honestly think he'd believe anything Damian said?'

Byron's sigh was resigned. 'No, I guess not. I'll have a talk to Nathan myself once he's calmed down a bit.'

'I don't like your chances, either. The man has no trust in him. Gemma tells me he's always treated her like a child, or a possession, that he never confides in her or talks to her about things that matter. She still loves the man but she was terribly hurt by his keeping my identity from her. I'm not sure she'll ever forgive him for that.'

'Time has a way of lessening such hurts, Celeste,' Byron said with the wisdom of age. 'I'm sure there were times when you thought you would never forgive me. Yet here you are, sitting in my car, going home to have dinner at Belleview.'

Celeste slowly nodded her head up and down. 'Yes, you're absolutely right. I shouldn't make harsh judgements of other people and their relationships. We're about to make history, I would say, when we announce our intention to marry. I'm sure a few people are going to faint dead away, my own mother included. I'm just thankful she's overseas at the moment. My God, the things I said to her about you. Still, it was my love turned to hate that kept me going when things were so tough. If I hadn't had my vows of vengeance I think I might have killed myself.'

'Oh, no, Celeste. You would never have killed yourself. You're a fighter, and fighters don't know any other way then to come out of their corners with all guns blazing. You sure blazed a path through my life over the years, madam. Whitmore's almost went to the wall because of you.'

Celeste had the grace to colour guiltily. 'I might have overstepped the mark occasionally.'

'That's putting it mildly. But I forgive you,' he grinned, 'provided you agree to some treaty terms.'

'Treaty terms? What do you think this is, Little Big Horn? And which side are you on? Colonel Custer's or the Indians'?'

'Whatever side won. Now on to the rules of truce.' He slanted her a quick glance. 'I suppose it would be too much to hope that you would hand over control of Campbell's to an impartial manager and retire to graceful living as my wife and social hostess.'

'You wish!' she laughed.

'Just as I thought. In that case I have to insist you stop using unfair and illegal business practices. If I find that Damian has—'

'Damian has been sacked from his position as sales and marketing manager,' she interrupted firmly. 'There will be no more shady goings-on at that level, I can assure you.'

'That's all I wanted to hear. Right! Now on to problem number two. Where are we going to live?'

'Certainly not in that imitation Southern mansion of yours!'

'Surely you don't expect me to reside in that crumbling castle *you* call home!'

They both looked at each other and laughed.

'We'll buy a brand-new place together,' Byron suggested, smiling.

'Only if I pay half,' Celeste argued.

'Agreed! It'll have to have a gym.'

'*And* a pool,' she put in.

'And I'd like to be by the sea for a change.'

'Good idea. It'll give me somewhere to put my boat.'

Byron scowled. 'I'd forgotten about that monstrosity. I'll bet it costs a fortune to run.'

'Mmm, it certainly does. Perhaps I should sell it. What do you think?'

'It's up to you.'

Celeste gave him a surprised look. 'You certainly have changed, haven't you? That's a most unByron-like answer.'

'You're going to be a most unByron-like wife,' he drawled. 'Maybe I should buy you a chastity-belt for a wedding present.'

She laughed. 'That cuts both ways, lover. Maybe I'll get *you* one.'

'After having you in my bed every night, I'll be lucky to make it to the office, let alone have the energy to consider extra-curricular activities.'

'From memory, you can be a very bad boy in offices.'

He groaned. 'Don't remind me. I still can't believe the sort of things we got up to that last week.'

'*We* got up to? Everything was *your* idea, might I remind you. You led and I simply followed.'

'There are followers and followers, Celeste,' he said drily. 'Your brand of following is something else. It's one of the reasons I thought you were more experienced than you were.'

'I loved you, Byron. I wanted to please you.'

'Hey, why the past tense? Don't you still love me and want to please me?'

'Silly man...' A lump filled her throat as their eyes locked for a moment.

'It's been a long time, hasn't it?' he said softly, but with a catch in his voice. 'But you've been worth the wait, my love. I hope you feel the same way about me.'

Celeste was incapable of answering. She let her blurred gaze do the talking and Byron's hand reached out for hers across the gear-stick. When she entwined her trembling fingers with his and he gave them a squeeze, her heart squeezed tight with them. It had indeed been a long hard journey, but at long last they were together. They were where they had always belonged. Her vows of vengeance would soon become a different kind of vow, one that would promise to love this man for the rest of her life.

When his hand had to leave hers to negotiate a corner she settled back into the seat with a happy sigh. Aside from her own personal happiness, it felt great to be going to give Gemma good news. Hopefully, their daughter would be pleased that her parents were going to be married. Maybe it would make up a little for her distress over the break-up of her own marriage. Celeste certainly hoped so.

'I STILL CAN'T believe it!' Ava said for the umpteenth time over dinner. 'It was enough of a shock when Gemma came home earlier and announced that you two were her parents, but now that I've heard the whole fantastic story I'm... I'm speechless!'

'For a person who's speechless, Ava,' Byron said drily, 'you've been saying one heck of a lot.' He suspected she might not be so chatty if she'd heard the whole unvarnished truth. But he and Celeste had decided that nothing would be gained by revealing the brutal treatment Celeste had suffered at the hands of that madman. It was to be thanked that he hadn't mistreated Gemma over the years. Clearly, he had loved the girl. But who wouldn't? It was impossible not to love such a loving creature. Not a word of criticism had she uttered against him and his treatment of her mother. He'd been accepted as unconditionally as Celeste had been.

'Very funny, Byron,' Ava retorted archly. 'You know what I mean. By the way, have you told Jade?'

Everyone at the table stopped eating, their mouths dropping open.

'She *has* just acquired a sister, hasn't she?'

'My God, so she has!' Byron said in a stunned voice.

Gemma's stomach had flipped over. A sister! She'd always wanted a sister. Not only that, Jade was expecting a baby, which meant she was going to become an aunt soon as well.

'I'll go and call her straight away,' Byron said, scraping his chair back and standing up. 'Maybe she and Kyle would like to drive over later and we can break open a bottle of champagne or two.'

'What a good idea,' Celeste said, then added mischievously, 'I wouldn't mind seeing that gorgeous hunk of a husband of hers at close range again.'

Byron glared down at her. 'I can see I'll be purchasing that CB before long,' he muttered darkly.

'CB?' Ava looked puzzled. 'What's a CB?'

'I have no idea,' Celeste said with mock bewilderment. 'What's a CB, Byron?'

Byron made an exasperated sound and strode from the room.

Ava shook her head after him. 'You have my admiration, Celeste, for having anything at all to do with that man! There are times when I'd like nothing better than to give him a swift kick up the backside.'

'I'll keep that in mind, Ava. So tell me all about that gorgeous hunk *you* seem to have snaffled for yourself. Have you met him, Gemma?'

Gemma, who'd been wondering how Jade would take the news, snapped back to the present. 'What was that?'

'Have you met Ava's fiancé?'

'No, I haven't yet. But he's dropping by later, isn't he, Ava?'

'Yes, I see him just about every night.'

Celeste noted the tinge of pink that immediately came to Ava's cheeks and she only just stopped her eyebrows from lifting. Apparently, therefore, it would be wise not to barge into Ava's room during any of this Vince's nightly visits.

'And when are you getting married?' Celeste asked.

'We've put the arrangements in Vince's mother's hands, and she's having a field-day. At the moment, we've made a tentative date for February next year. It seems it takes a while to organise an Italian wedding.'

'I can imagine.'

Byron strode back into the dining-room, a broad smile on his face. 'Jade's over the moon, Gemma. Frankly, I'm surprised I'm not deaf, she carried on so much. But I let her scream and cry and do all the things Jade likes doing. Anyway, she said she'd be over straight away.'

'Not alone, I hope,' Celeste quipped.

When Byron's blue eyes narrowed, she laughed, and leant over to kiss him on the cheek. 'You can't expect me to give up teasing you altogether, can you? You do jealousy better than any man I know.'

Would you believe Vince gets jealous of *me*?' Ava said, sounding almost surprised. 'I think jealousy must be an infallible symptom of a man's love. If he doesn't get jealous at all then he probably doesn't care.'

'In that case, I must care for Celeste one hell of a lot,' Byron drawled. 'When another man even *looks* her way, I want to punch his lights out.'

'Must be the beast in you, darling,' Celeste murmured, and looked adoringly at him.

'Any man worth his salt has a bit of beast in him,' Byron returned. What woman wants a wimp, especially these days? He has to stand up and be counted, I say.'

'Hear, hear!' Celeste clapped.

'Vince can be a beast when necessary, can't he, Byron?' Ava said smilingly.

He gave his sister a rueful look and rubbed his jaw. 'He's certainly not a man to be toyed with.'

'Unless Ava's doing the toying,' Celeste murmured, bringing a startled look from Byron and a coy half-smile from Ava.

Gemma listened to this exchange, her thoughts whirling as the conversation reconfirmed what, in her heart, she already knew. Nathan did love her. Madly. Obsessively. He'd been thrown by her inexplicably leaving him, then distraught when he thought she'd run to Damian. Crazed by jealousy, he had done what others would decry as an unthinkable act, but she'd already accepted that the assault had been a momentary aberration, a temporary insanity which he had immediately regretted.

But Gemma's belief that her husband really loved her did not change the fact that he did not believe she loved him. He'd said so, told her she was too young for such depth of emotion, confessing that he'd selfishly rushed her into marriage on her response to a strong sexual attraction. This was the reason he'd treated her as he had, buying her gifts all the time, cosseting and smothering her as an insecure older lover might do to a Lolita-style mistress, fearful all the time that she would grow bored and leave him. He'd deliberately kept the focus of the relationship on sex because that was the area he was most confident in, his role becoming a mixture of father and Svengali.

It was in the father role that he made decisions for her all the time, especially the one not to tell her who her mother was, probably because he felt a mother like Celeste would be like his own mother, and consequently not worth knowing. The Svengali role was that of seducer and enslaver, taking her desire for him and exploiting it to the full, attuning her body to his needs so finely that she had seemed to lose some of her will power in that regard. He could sometimes make her respond even when she didn't feel she wanted to.

Who knew? Maybe Nathan had thought the other day that she would even respond to his forced act of intercourse. Of course she hadn't, and when he'd finally seen that, she gained the impression that he was filled with remorse and self-disgust.

But all this thinking left her where? Nathan insisted he didn't want her back as his wife, obviously because of her supposed adultery. How he could believe she'd go from him to Damian so soon after their very loving phone call on the previous Friday night was beyond her.

How happy she had been after that phone call. And
how optimistic for the future. She hadn't been able to
wait to throw away her pills, to come home to Nathan
and to...

Gemma froze as the possibility struck. Dear God, she
had never thought of that. The idea that she might have
conceived a child that awful afternoon seemed a wicked
twist of fate, but it was a distinct possibility, maybe even
a probability!

Gemma blinked as the idea took hold. Why wasn't she
appalled by the thought? Or disgusted? Or revolted?

Because she wasn't, that was why. Any child resulting
from that unfortunate union would still be the offspring
of two people who loved one another, however mis-
guided one of them was.

'Gemma?' Celeste asked. 'Are you all right?'

Lord, but she was finding it hard not to actually feel
excited by this, which was crazy! Looking up, she struggled for composure. 'Yes. I'm fine. Why?

'You ... you looked strange for a moment.'

I not only look strange, Mother, I *am* strange, Gemma
decided. Any other woman would be horrified. But not
silly old optimistic me. Because even if I'm *not* pregnant, this has shown me what having a child of Nathan's
means to me, what *Nathan* means to me.

It looks as if I'm going to have to win him back, came
the astonishing realisation. By fair means or foul, if necessary. He's not going to get away from me, she decided
with a surge of steely spirit. I'm not going to do what
Celeste did with Byron. Nathan is the man for me and
he's the man for me *here and now*, not in twenty years'
time.

I have a weapon or two in my favour, Gemma planned
with quite amazing calm. My body for one. Nathan does
have an addiction for it. On top of that, he actually loves
me. Lust plus love is a pretty powerful and potentially
weakening combination. If I'm not pregnant this time,
I'm certainly going to become so in the not too distant
future.

And then ... *then* ...

Gemma grimaced at this point in her train of thought. She couldn't think that far ahead. She'd have to take this plan one day at a time.

'Gemma?' Celeste asked again.

She looked up to find everyone looking at her with concerned expressions on their faces. 'Sorry, I was day-dreaming, making plans for the future.'

Now everyone looked even more taken aback.

'I can keep my job at the store, can't I, Byron?' she asked.

'Of course!'

'And I . . . I'd like to stay living here, if I could.' Nathan was more likely to come to Belleview than Campbell Court, she reasoned. 'I hope you're not offended, Mother. I'll visit you as well.'

'You do what you think best, Gemma, love. You're a grown woman.'

'Then I think it best I stay here. Damian won't be annoyed, will he?'

'Your *uncle* Damian will understand,' Celeste said firmly.

'My goodness, so he is! I didn't think of that.'

'You've also acquired a grandmother,' Celeste added, 'who's going to come home like a shot once she finds out.'

'A grandmother too!' Gemma gasped. 'Gosh, it's hard to take it all in.'

'It's been quite a day, I have to admit,' Byron intoned drily just as the doorbell rang. 'And it hasn't finished yet. Come on, Gemma, I need moral support to let that mad sister of yours in.'

'Gemma laughed and stood up. 'I never thought I'd see the day when you'd become a scaredy-cat.'

'Well, take a good look, daughter, dear, because come tomorrow I'm going to revert to normal.'

And come tomorrow, she promised herself as she linked arms with her father and walked from the room, I'm going to set about getting my Nathan back!

HARLEQUIN®

Don't miss these Harlequin favorites by some of our most
distinguished authors!
And now you can receive a discount by ordering two or more titles!

HT#25593	WHAT MIGHT HAVE BEEN by Glenda Sanders	$2.99 U.S. ☐ /$3.50 CAN. ☐
HP#11713	AN UNSUITABLE WIFE by Lindsay Armstrong	$2.99 U.S. ☐ /$3.50 CAN. ☐
HR#03356	BACHELOR'S FAMILY by Jessica Steele	$2.99 U.S.☐ /$3.50 CAN. ☐
HS#70494	THE BIG SECRET by Janice Kaiser	$3.39 ☐
HI#22196	CHILD'S PLAY by Bethany Campbell	$2.89 ☐
HAR#16553	THE MARRYING TYPE by Judith Arnold	$3.50 U.S. ☐ /$3.99 CAN. ☐
HH#28844	THE TEMPTING OF JULIA by Maura Seger	$3.99 U.S ☐ /$4.50 CAN. ☐

(limited quantities available on certain titles)

AMOUNT	$
DEDUCT: 10% DISCOUNT FOR 2+ BOOKS	$
POSTAGE & HANDLING ($1.00 for one book, 50¢ for each additional)	$
APPLICABLE TAXES*	$_____
TOTAL PAYABLE	$_____

(check or money order—please do not send cash)

To order, complete this form and send it, along with a check or money order for the
total above, payable to Harlequin Books, to: **In the U.S.:** 3010 Walden Avenue,
P.O. Box 9047, Buffalo, NY 14269-9047; **In Canada:** P.O. Box 613, Fort Erie, Ontario,
L2A 5X3.

Name: _____

Address:_____City: _____

State/Prov.: _____ Zip/Postal Code: _____

*New York residents remit applicable sales taxes.
 Canadian residents remit applicable GST and provincial taxes.

HBACK-OD2

HARLEQUIN PRESENTS®

Dark secrets...

forbidden desires...

scandalous discoveries...

an enthralling six-part saga from a bright new talent!

HEARTS OF FIRE
by Miranda Lee

This exciting family saga is set in the glamorous world of
opal dealing in Australia. *HEARTS OF FIRE* unfolds over
six books, revealing the passion, scandal, sin and hope
that exist between two fabulously rich families. Each novel
features its own gripping romance—and you'll also be
hooked by the continuing story of Gemma Smith's search
for the truth about her real mother, and the priceless
Black Opal....

Coming next month:

The story concludes with

BOOK 6: *Marriage & Miracles*

Gemma's marriage to Nathan couldn't be over! There was
so much that was unresolved between them.... And, most
importantly, Gemma was still in love with Nathan. She also
had an extraspecial secret to share with her husband—she
was expecting his baby.

Harlequin Presents: you'll want to know what happens next!

Available in December, wherever Harlequin books are sold.

HARLEQUIN PRESENTS®

Harlequin brings you the best books, by the best authors!

LYNNE GRAHAM

Bestselling author of *Indecent Deception*

&

SANDRA MARTON

"Sandra Marton aims for her readers' hearts."
—*Romantic Times*

Coming next month:

THE UNFAITHFUL WIFE by Lynne Graham
Harlequin Presents #1779

Leah wanted a divorce...but Nik didn't! Why *would*
Nik Andreakis want to hang on to the wife he'd been
blackmailed into marrying? And why—after ignoring
Leah for five long years—was Nik suddenly making
passionate advances toward her?

HOSTAGE OF THE HAWK by Sandra Marton
Harlequin Presents #1780

Surely Joanna should despise Khalil? After all...the man
was holding her hostage! But Joanna had found heaven in
Khalil's embrace and now she wanted more...much more
from her "Hawk of the North"....

Harlequin Presents—the best has just gotten better!
Available in December, wherever Harlequin books are sold.

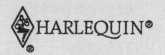

HARLEQUIN®

CHRISTMAS ROGUES

is giving you everything 🎄 **you want on
your Christmas list this year:**

✔️ -great romance stories

✔️ -award-winning authors

✔️ -a FREE gift promotion

✔️ -an abundance of Christmas cheer

This November, not only can you join ANITA MILLS,
PATRICIA POTTER and MIRANDA JARRETT
for exciting, heartwarming Christmas stories
about roguish men and the women who tame
them—but you can also receive a FREE gold-tone
necklace. (Details inside all copies of
Christmas Rogues.)

CHRISTMAS ROGUES—romance reading at its
best—only from HARLEQUIN BOOKS!

**Available in November wherever
Harlequin books are sold.**